A Body in the Attic

A Myrtle Clover Cozy Mystery, Volume 16

Elizabeth Spann Craig

Published by Elizabeth Spann Craig, 2020.

A BODY IN THE ATTIC

First edition. May 21, 2020.

Written by Elizabeth Spann Craig.

Chapter One

"You have to play by the rules," said Miles coldly.

Myrtle looked up from the chess board. "I thought I *was* playing by the rules."

Miles pushed his glasses up his nose and looked solemnly at her. "You know that you can't move the rook like that."

"You mean the castle?" Myrtle peered down at the offending chess piece. "This is precisely why this game is ridiculous, Miles. A rook isn't a castle. The piece should resemble a large crow, instead."

"Regardless, it doesn't move like you just moved it."

Myrtle sighed and put the rook back where it came from. "We should be playing Scrabble. Scrabble makes sense."

"Chess makes sense. It just doesn't make sense the way you play it. Besides, we agreed to take a break from Scrabble."

Myrtle glared at the chess board. "I didn't actually agree to take a break from Scrabble. And I really don't enjoy this game."

"Only because it's not a word game. And because it's occurring to you that you might not win," said Miles.

"There's nothing wrong with being competitive. I can't help it that I'm so good at Scrabble that no one wants to play with me." Myrtle looked contrary.

"I've told you that what you need to do is play Scrabble with your computer. The computer will always play with you and might actually have a chance to win," said Miles.

Myrtle shrugged. "I don't think I would have the same sense of satisfaction at beating the computer." She studied the chessboard for a moment and smoothly took Miles's bishop.

Miles frowned, leaning close to the board to study the move Myrtle just made. Then he sighed and took off his glasses, cleaning them with his pristine handkerchief. "You distracted me on purpose with the whole rook thing."

"I did no such thing. I simply pointed out that it was a silly name for the chess piece."

Miles gave her a suspicious look, as if Myrtle might be much better at chess than she was letting on. "Let's take a break. We can pick the game up later."

They were playing in Miles's living room. They'd discovered Myrtle's house was dangerous for playing games in. Sometimes Myrtle's feral cat Pasha decided to sit on the game board and knock pieces around. Sometimes Myrtle's housekeeper Puddin would lackadaisically vacuum and destroy the board in the process.

"Not only is it time for a break, it's time for *Tomorrow's Promise*. And it's perfect timing. You've become obsessed with chess and we shouldn't feed into your obsession." Myrtle pushed her chair back and dropped into one of the armchairs facing Miles's television. The soap opera, with all its unlikely storylines and overacting, was her favorite show and Miles's guilty pleasure.

"Not obsessed. Just interested. And I'm wanting to build my skills again since it's been a while since I played."

"You're so *competitive*, Miles!"

Miles shook his head and turned on the television. "Not really. I just don't want to embarrass myself completely against Darren. He knows I used to be in the chess club in high school."

Myrtle arched her eyebrows. "And how did he discover that fascinating tidbit of information?"

Miles colored a little. "I might have mentioned it in a passing moment. It was a mistake. He annihilated me during our first couple of games together and I'm trying to ensure our next game is a little more competitive." He frowned. "Where did the remote go?"

"How inconvenient. How could you lose anything in a house this tidy?"

Miles narrowed his eyes at his favorite armchair and spotted a bit of black plastic poking up from the side of the cushion. "There it is." He pointed the errant remote at the television and frowned again as nothing happened.

"It seems as if the world is conspiring to keep us from watching our soap," said Myrtle in irritation. "Isn't there a way to manually change the channel on this TV?"

"If there is, I don't know about it." Miles adjusted his glasses again and studied the television.

"For heaven's sake: you were a computer programmer. Surely you can figure out your new television." Myrtle stood up herself, giving the device a mistrustful look. "This is exactly why I keep my old television set from twenty years ago. It *always* allows me to watch shows and it has clearly marked buttons so I can change channels even if the remote is AWOL. And it sits perfectly on my little stand. This behemoth seems to have taken complete control here."

"I was an engineer," said Miles through gritted teeth. "And the problem has to do with the remote being out of batteries. There's nothing wrong with the television."

"There's nothing right with it, either." Myrtle plopped back down in her armchair.

Miles pulled open a drawer in his desk and peered dolefully inside. "Out of batteries? I swear I bought some just a few weeks ago."

Myrtle shook her head. "I can see *Tomorrow's Promise* is simply not meant to be."

"We can go to the store and buy batteries. You always need things from the store anyway. Or we can watch the show at your house."

Myrtle said, "At this point, we should concede defeat. I don't want to interfere with fate. If we're not supposed to watch our soap opera today, we should watch it tomorrow." She clasped her hands in her lap and said, "What else is on the agenda?"

Miles sat back down in the armchair next to her. "Nothing, really. We've played chess. We tried to watch our show. I suppose we could go for lunch at Bo's Diner."

"But we had snacks during chess. I'm not a bit hungry yet."

Miles considered their quandary. It was a small town. The options were limited. "A walk? We haven't taken a walk for a while."

"Erma is at home. She's sure to foist herself on us and make us listen while she talks about her latest gruesome medical problem."

"She might be out running errands." Miles stood up and cautiously opened his front door to look out. He made a face and sat back down again.

Myrtle sighed. "I'm overdue for an Erma encounter and I don't want to have it today. I think she's staying inside and planning her attack."

Miles's phone rang and he pulled it out of his pocket.

"Oh, hi, Darren," said Miles.

Myrtle sighed. It would be most inconvenient if Darren wanted to play chess with Miles now. Chess wasn't very interesting even as a participant. It would be much less interesting as an observer.

"No, I'm not doing anything important now."

Myrtle rolled her eyes.

"All right. Sure. I have Myrtle with me, is that okay?" Miles glanced over at Myrtle. "We'll come over in a little bit. Thanks."

"I really hope that wasn't an invitation to play chess with Darren," said Myrtle.

Miles shook his head. "Darren wanted to talk about something interesting in his attic. Something to do with old clippings and somebody named Liam. He asked if we could run by."

"Well, that does actually sound somewhat more intriguing than taking a walk with Erma, so let's do it." Myrtle stood up and frowned as she brushed a few errant popcorn bits off her slacks. "Did he say what he'd found? Is it more in the order of an old newspaper with steaks selling for 40 cents? Surely he didn't discover another art find that needs to go to *Antique Roadshow* for evaluation?"

"He didn't say." Miles picked up his keys from his desk and frowned at an envelope there. "Oh, no. I meant to put this in my mailbox this morning. Has the mail come already?"

"Two hours ago, right on time," said Myrtle. She kept track of things like that. If there was one thing she wasn't a fan of, it was mail carriers or garbage collectors who didn't come at their regularly scheduled time.

Miles looked alarmed. "I really needed this to go out today. I'm paying a bill."

"Couldn't you pay it online?"

"Not without paying their service fee. And that really annoys me. I shouldn't have to pay a fee for the pleasure of paying a bill."

Myrtle said, "Don't be so agitated, Miles! We'll simply go to the post office first and drop it in the box. Darren can wait for the few minutes it takes to do that. I doubt whatever he's found in his attic is going to go anywhere in that amount of time."

"I suppose not," said Miles slowly. "He did say he needed to make a phone call."

So they ran Miles's post office errand. But then Myrtle pointed out they might as well get batteries for the remote since they were out already. They were accosted by a couple of people from Myrtle's garden club who flirted with Miles while Myrtle glared at her watch. Finally, Miles drove to Darren's house.

Chapter Two

Unfortunately, Darren was beyond needing help.

Myrtle's police chief son, Red, arrived, shaking his head at the sight of his mother. "Y'all wait outside, please. Maybe in Miles's car? I need to talk with the EMT and paramedic." Miles pointed him in the direction of the attic and he set off.

Myrtle frowned as she saw Miles walking a bit unsteadily in the direction of his car. He also blinked several times rapidly. A distraction appeared to be in order. That, or she'd have to surrender her cane to Miles for the sake of his own stability.

Myrtle said in a confiding tone, "What do you think about Red?"

Miles looked confused. "About Red? In what way?"

"Have you noticed how very gray he's looking lately? The color of Red's hair used to be the entire reason for his nickname." Myrtle opened the passenger door and sat inside.

"Are the gray hairs because of you? Have you been giving Red a hard time lately?" asked Miles, slowly, his mind still on his friend's death.

"A hard time? Me? Certainly not. That is, not that *much* of a hard time."

"No shenanigans at Greener Pastures?" asked Miles. The color appeared to be slowly coming back to his face.

Myrtle snorted. "I've been *very helpful* over there. I assisted the inmates in writing an editorial letter to the paper to address some of the issues at the retirement home."

"I'm sure Red loved that," said Miles. Red's fondest wish was to have his octogenarian mother safely ensconced in the hallowed walls of Greener Pastures. Myrtle, however, had no plans for living there. "And they're residents, not inmates."

"Tell them that. They feel like inmates. The best part was the banner," said Myrtle thoughtfully. She glanced across at Miles. "That's the thing these days—visuals are so important."

Miles frowned. "I didn't realize editorials had photographs with them."

"They don't, at least not in the *Bradley Bugle*. No, the pictures were for social media. It proved quite the effective approach." Myrtle gave a pleased, smile at the memory. "I brought black paint and a large paint brush. The inmates painted 'help' on a sheet and hung it out a couple of windows while I took pictures below. You wouldn't believe the number of shares it had online."

The corners of Miles's eyes crinkled. "Oh, I think I can guess."

Myrtle pursed her lips. "Anyway, the administrator there called Red. Most annoying. And, I thought, a direct violation of their rights as Americans."

"Freedom to gather?" asked Miles.

"And freedom of speech. Probably more freedoms than that, too. Red was most displeased about the whole thing."

"About curtailing their rights?" Miles pushed his glasses up his nose.

"Oh, no. Not at all. No, he was displeased about my involvement in a viral post involving Greener Pastures. He seems to think I'll never get admitted there now." Myrtle smirked and watched as her aforementioned son walked out of Darren's house, pulling out his notebook as he came. "Goodness, I think he's looking a little pudgy now, too. Hmm."

Red stopped in front of them, tapping his pen on his notebook. "Mama, I'm going to pass on speaking with you about this right now. I'm assuming Miles was the one who was in the attic and discovered Darren?"

Miles swallowed and nodded, wordlessly.

Red's voice became gentler. "Can I get you something to drink? Water, maybe? I have a small cooler in my car with some water bottles."

Miles gave him a grateful look and Red hurried off for the water.

Myrtle muttered huffily, "I have important information, too. My *impressions* of things are always very useful."

Red returned with the water and patiently waited as Miles carefully unscrewed the top and drank several gulps.

Miles nodded again at Red to indicate he'd be fine to keep going.

"All right. First off, how do you know Darren? Y'all play Scrabble together?"

Miles gave Myrtle a sideways look. "Um, no. I've decided to curtail my Scrabble-playing."

Red said in an easy tone, "I can only imagine. Playing Scrabble with my mother isn't exactly a walk in the park. And not great for one's ego, either."

Myrtle gave an annoyed cluck and Red continued, "So not Scrabble then."

Miles shook his head. "It was chess." He cleared his throat and his voice was a bit stronger. "Darren and I played chess together. He was very good."

Red jotted down a note. "So you two were going to play chess this morning. And Mama came over as a sort of cheerleader?" A corner of his lips pulled up in a smile.

Myrtle gave him a withering look and pointedly turned to stare out the window.

"Actually, we weren't going to play chess today. Darren called me unexpectedly and asked me to come over. He'd found something in his attic."

Red looked a lot more alert. "Something in the attic? Did he say what?"

Miles shook his head. "Not really. Some sort of clippings."

Red glanced at his watch. "And y'all called me right after you found him?"

"That's right." Miles hesitated and then looked guilty. "But we didn't drive directly over to Darren's house after he called."

Myrtle said firmly, "Miles, it was practically direct."

"No, we had to go in the opposite direction to drop off a bill payment at the post office," said Miles miserably. "Then we ran by the store."

Red, for once, agreed with Myrtle. "It wasn't like you headed over there hours later, Miles. We're talking about . . . what? Twenty minutes later?"

"I should have been here sooner," said Miles sadly. "Maybe I could have done CPR or something."

Red tapped his pen against his notebook again. "Sorry?"

Miles tilted his head slightly. "Well . . . it looked to me as if Darren had suffered a heart attack. He's not young and he's talked about being on heart medicine."

Red sighed. "Miles, I'm sorry to tell you this, but Darren was murdered."

Myrtle sat up a bit straighter.

Miles stared at him, wide-eyed. "I didn't . . . well, I didn't notice a wound."

"It was on the back of his head and then he fell backwards. It looks as though he was hit with that heavy-duty flashlight he had up there with him. Which neither of you needs to tell anyone about." Red gave Miles a serious look. "So don't be feeling guilty about not being here any earlier. If you and Mama *had* been here just a little sooner, y'all might be dead as well."

Miles shivered and Myrtle snorted. "I'd have beaten the villain with my cane within an inch of his life. The very idea of killing Darren! What on earth did he ever do to anybody?"

Red looked serious. "That's what I'd very much like to find out. And he didn't give you any indication of what he'd found, Miles?"

Miles shook his head. "Just clippings and something about someone named Liam."

"Liam Hudson?" asked Red sharply.

Miles shrugged. "I don't know any Liams."

"He's a lawyer here in town," said Myrtle.

Miles said, "He didn't say which Liam."

"There surely can't be too many of them floating around," said Myrtle.

Red said, "I did notice someone appeared to have gone through the attic. It must have happened very quickly. His attic looked messy to me and the rest of his house was neat and tidy."

Miles said, "It looked odd to me, too. I'm sure Darren would have kept his attic just as organized as the rest of his house."

Red tapped his pen against his notebook again. "Do you have any idea if anyone was upset with Darren? Had he had any run-ins with anyone recently? Issues?"

Miles frowned. "He did mention some things. But I was mostly focused on my next chess move, I'm afraid."

"For heaven's sake," groaned Myrtle from the backseat.

Miles drew his eyebrows together. "Let's see. I might be able to come up with something. It must sound as if I wasn't listening to Darren at all." He looked guilty again.

Red said soothingly, "I get it—you were trying not to be distracted while you figured out your next move. Darren must have been a very good player."

Miles nodded. "That's right."

Red said, "Maybe if you did a quick rundown of his relationships. That might help me get started."

Miles said slowly, "Let's see. He's dating Pansy Denham. But they get along really well."

Red gave him a reassuring smile. "I'm just taking notes and gathering information. I'm not going to automatically suspect everyone in his circle of having murdered him."

Miles took a deep breath. "His sister, as you probably know, is Orabelle Whitley. She's our mail carrier."

"And a very good one," said Myrtle appreciatively. "Prompt and courteous."

Miles continued mulling Darren's connections over. "He does have a nephew . . . Orabelle's son. I can't remember his name. I believe Darren does sometimes have a few run-ins with him."

Red nodded, jotting this down. "What types of run-ins?"

"I think he's usually short on cash." Miles said this somewhat apologetically, as if getting Darren's unnamed nephew into trouble hadn't really been on his to-do list that day.

"Anyone else?" asked Red.

Miles shook his head. "I know there are others, but I can't for the life of me think who they are." He glanced through the windshield and said, "Oh no. Here comes Darren's sister."

Sure enough, the mail truck had pulled to the curb and Orabelle exited the vehicle, looking concerned.

Red straightened up. "I'll speak with her."

He swiftly strode over to the mail truck and gently helped Orabelle to sit down. Miles looked away as Orabelle's face crumpled at the news.

Myrtle said, "We should have lunch after this, Miles."

"I'm not hungry."

"Precisely why we should get you something to eat. Fried food will help you get over your shock," said Myrtle briskly.

Miles frowned. "Is that medically-sound advice?"

"Of course it is. Anyway, that's what we'll do as soon as we leave here."

Miles risked a glance through the windshield again and looked relieved to see that Orabelle had composed herself. "Oh. It looks like the state police are driving up."

Myrtle scooted forward to see better. "And Lieutenant Perkins is here!"

Detective Lieutenant Perkins with the state police was a favorite of Myrtle's. She'd even had him over for a memorable dinner once. What she liked best about him was the way he always listened and appreciated her opinion on his cases. As opposed to her son, she thought with a sniff.

Perkins spotted Myrtle in the car and gave her a wave and a smile before ducking quickly into the house as Red joined him.

Miles said, "It looks like Orabelle is coming over."

"You don't have to sound like you're about to get a cavity filled, Miles. We'll simply give her an abridged version of what happened this morning. Then maybe she can give us some information about who could have done this." Myrtle hopped out of the car and Miles slowly started following suit. Myrtle gave him a sharp look. "Are you sure you're okay, Miles? If you keel over, there's no way I'll be able to catch you. Want my cane?"

Miles said in a dignified voice, "I do not. I'm fine, thank you. And I should certainly stand in this particular circumstance."

"I've always liked Orabelle," said Myrtle. "Very prompt mail delivery. Always."

Miles rolled his eyes. "And she likely has other admirable qualities."

"I've never wanted to hold her up from her appointed rounds." As Orabelle reached them, Myrtle said, "Orabelle, we're so very sorry. Would you like to take a seat?" She gestured to Miles's recently vacated car.

Orabelle shook her head stiffly and seemed to be keeping rigid control of her emotions. "I'm good, thanks. It was quite a shock, but now I just want answers." Her eyes narrowed. "And, possibly, revenge."

Myrtle reflected that Orabelle looked to be the type of person to enact it, too. She was a stern-looking woman who had, Myrtle recalled, a tendency to bark at people. Her gray hair was held back in a no-nonsense headband. Myrtle, at right around six feet tall, was accustomed to looking down at the tops of women's heads, but Orabelle could look her in the eye.

Myrtle said, "Well, Miles and I are just terribly sorry." Miles nodded and Myrtle continued. "I know you've been out delivering the mail. You didn't happen to see anything suspicious when you drove by, I suppose?"

Orabelle said, "As a matter of fact, I was home today with the day off. One of my coworkers delivered today." She glanced across the yard as some suited forensics workers entered Darren's house. Orabelle shivered.

Myrtle raised her eyebrows in surprise. "I'm really surprised to hear that. My mail was delivered precisely on time and that so rarely happens unless you're delivering."

Orabelle gave her a small smile. "Yes, well, Mary Lynn is getting better all the time. But she did work today. I'm just driving the truck to run an errand so I haven't been by the house at all." She added with no slight degree of emphasis, "And Tripp was at home with me, too. You remember my son, Tripp. I think you taught him."

Myrtle thought she remembered Tripp as rather lazy and sassy. But she nodded instead.

"He's living with me on a temporary basis, you know. He's planning on going back to school," said Orabelle, pride momentarily replacing the sorrow on her face.

"That's wonderful," said Myrtle, meaning it. She wasn't entirely sure what school Tripp had originally forfeited his degree at, but it had to be better that he was returning to finish it up.

Orabelle turned, distracted by the state police speaking to each other and stringing police tape across the front of the property.

"Poor Darren," she said in a soft voice. "He simply didn't deserve this."

Miles apparently was able to dredge at least one memory from the depths of his brain. He said, "He didn't. And I thought his luck had turned for the better, after discovering that painting in his attic. He said it had turned out to be fairly lucrative, I believe."

Myrtle stifled a sigh. Miles was clearly spending too much time thinking about chess and not nearly enough thinking about fascinating attic finds of recently-murdered friends.

Orabelle gave him a sharp look. She said in a careful voice, "Yes. Something like that. Of course it was a pleasant surprise for Darren. You know how he loves discoveries of *any* kind. He was forever telling me about things he'd come across and really enjoyed. He'd just listened to Mozart's Masonic Funeral march and loved it." She gave a dry laugh that had a bit of a sob in it.

"He wouldn't allow me *not* to listen to it. And it was beautiful and only six minutes long. Maybe I should have it playing at his service as people arrive."

Miles looked uncomfortable and somewhat guilty again as the mention of Darren's funeral was broached. But Myrtle was reflecting on the fact that Orabelle had very effectively changed the subject.

Orabelle said, "Now, if you could, would both of you fill me in a little more as to what happened this morning? How did you end up being in Darren's attic?"

Myrtle lifted her cane and said, "Well, I wasn't in his attic, but Miles was."

Miles shifted on his feet. "Yes. Darren called and invited me to come over. I thought at first perhaps he wanted us to play chess again, but he'd found something of interest in his attic again and wanted me to take a look." He pushed his glasses up his nose. "When he didn't answer the door, we went looking for him."

Orabelle gave a sniff and nodded sharply. "And Red said he was murdered. That it wasn't a natural death."

Miles said, "That's what he told us. But it wasn't obvious when I was up there with him. I'd originally thought he'd suffered a heart attack or a massive stroke."

"It must have been very quick," said Orabelle in a hopeful tone.

Myrtle said, "It didn't take us long to arrive here. It must have been very quick indeed."

Orabelle nodded again and her gaze drifted sadly over her brother's house. She seemed to pale a little as her eyes locked on something near Darren's front steps.

Miles seemed oblivious, still caught up in his thoughts, but Myrtle followed the direction of Orabelle's gaze. There were a pair of sunglasses lying there. They appeared to be quite youthful-looking ones, too, and nothing that Orabelle would dream of wearing. But judging from her expression, the sunglasses were important. Myrtle had the feeling they might belong to her son, Tripp.

At that moment, Lieutenant Perkins stepped outside with Red. He gave another polite wave to Myrtle and then his focus sharpened and he called to someone wearing an evidence suit. The pair of sunglasses was quickly zipped up into a plastic bag.

Orabelle seemed to deflate a little at this.

Myrtle said, "Orabelle, I understand Darren was seeing Pansy Denham."

Orabelle groaned. "Yes, he was. She'll be a disaster when she hears about this. I hope Red will tell her so I won't have to do the honors. I'm not in the right mindset to deal with hysteria."

Myrtle said, "Pansy can be rather emotional, can't she? I don't know her as well as you likely do. What's she like?"

"I never warmed to her," said Orabelle promptly. "And Darren told me the two of them hadn't been on the best of terms lately. Not to suggest that Pansy had anything to do with this, of course."

"Goodness," said Myrtle, adopting her fluffy, gossipy old lady persona, "what happened between the two of them?" She leaned in as if hanging on Orabelle's every word.

Orabelle shook her head. "That I don't know. Only that Darren told me they'd had a few issues. I can hazard a guess, though. You know how Darren treasured his quiet time."

"He was quite the reader, as I recall. He and I would chat about books sometimes," said Myrtle.

"Exactly. And he liked quiet pursuits like chess," said Orabelle with a nod at Miles. "And lately, he'd enjoyed spending a good deal of time in his attic, messing about. But Pansy seemed jealous of the time he'd spend alone, in the attic, or playing chess. She was quite irritated about it. Darren would be all comfy inside with a good book and Pansy would insist he take her to dinner or out to the movies. She's a very persistent woman." Orabelle tightened her lips into a thin line as if persistence wasn't a quality she particularly admired.

They stopped speaking as Red approached them. Red gave Orabelle a kind smile and said, "Unfortunately, there's nothing you can do here. I think our team will be here for a while. Why don't you go home and get some rest?"

Orabelle gave a quick nod and then briskly asked, "Will you be informing Pansy Denham?"

Red said, "He was dating her, wasn't he? Yes, we'll let her know." He looked tired as he glanced over at Myrtle. "Mama, you should head home, too."

"Won't you need to speak with Miles again?" asked Myrtle.

"I think I got all the information I need from him right now," said Red firmly. He glanced over at Miles. "Why don't y'all head over to Bo's Diner and have lunch? Miles looks a little peaked."

Myrtle was cross at being dismissed from the crime scene, but Miles definitely wasn't looking so hot and she needed her sidekick in tip-top condition. "Sure," she said reluctantly.

One of the state police called to Red and he hurried away.

Chapter Three

M iles turned a bit green at the thought of the diner. "I'm not sure fried food would sit well on my stomach right now."

"They have plenty of other options," said Myrtle. "You know you usually end up with a salad over there. Besides, Red wants us to leave and he'll continue glaring at me until we do."

Miles was finally, and reluctantly, convinced and soon they were walking into Bo's Diner in downtown Bradley. The restaurant hadn't changed in decades with its vinyl booths, laminated menus, and linoleum flooring.

Before long, Myrtle was contentedly eating a pimento cheese hot dog and French fries. Miles looked askance at her plate and pushed around salad greens without any of them actually getting put into his mouth.

Myrtle watched him for a moment as she took a sip of her iced tea. "You're not really going to get any nutritional benefits that way, you know. The food must be digested. You're just pushing it into the corners of your plate to make it appear you've eaten something."

Miles sighed. "I'm just not that hungry."

"Thinking about Darren again?" asked Myrtle.

Miles nodded and Myrtle pursed her lips in thought. "As a matter of fact, there's one thing I can distract you with. I'd like to discuss something with you."

Miles frowned. "That sounds ominous."

"Oh, it's perfectly fine, Miles. It's just that I need you to go to book club with me tomorrow afternoon."

Miles pushed his salad so far to the edge of the plate that a bit hit the table. He scowled at it.

Myrtle continued, "You haven't been to the last three meetings. It's a source of some concern with the ladies. You know how you brighten their day by being there."

Myrtle smirked and Miles rolled his eyes at her. He said, "It's a little dispiriting to attend book club when there are only ten minutes allotted to the chosen book. And, frankly, when the allotted book isn't even worth ten minutes."

"I'd agree. But you know your methods aren't exactly helpful. We have to *ease* into literature with that club and those women. You practically killed book club when you introduced *The Mayor of Casterbridge*."

Miles sighed. "I can tell you have a plan."

"I do. I already changed the book club meeting this month to the library's community room to remind everyone that our club is about *books*." Myrtle sat back in the booth and beamed at Miles.

Miles said grudgingly, "It might work. But you realize the problem with that approach is the alcohol. The library won't allow it. The rest of book club won't want to show up if it means giving up their vodka and tonics. Attendance might be very low."

Myrtle said in a severe voice, "The book club has become entirely too tipsy in recent months. I believe a drying out stretch might be best. Besides, we can still have food in the community room and the snacks are also popular. And that's another reason why I need you to come. Like I mentioned, you're a big draw."

"I haven't read the book."

"Believe me, Miles, *no one* has read the book. Probably not even Tippy, who proposed the silly thing. I have a good idea for the next book, though."

"*The Sound and the Fury?*" asked Miles hopefully.

"I'll overlook your little Faulkner obsession. There's no way book club can handle his streams of consciousness. They'll end up quite dizzy. No, I thought we should revert to high school English and try *House of Mirth*. I have the feeling the group will enjoy it. Or they won't read it, which will put us at the same point we are now. At any rate, nothing *bad* will happen with that particular book choice." Myrtle polished off the last bite of her hot dog.

"I suppose that will be fine," said Miles. "I do like Edith Wharton."

Myrtle said, "Well, thank goodness you'll come. I was concerned you'd drag your feet. I know how you don't like attending when you haven't read the selection." She knit her brows as Miles lay down his fork and left the salad untouched. "There's actually another reason I think you'll want to be at the meeting. Pansy Denham will be there."

Miles pushed his plate away. "She's not a member, is she? I haven't been gone *that* long."

"She's not, yet. But I think she's about to be. Tippy invited her. And, as a matter of fact, I believe Pansy is something of an anomaly for our group in that she appears to be an actual *reader*. Despite how silly she can appear sometimes, she actually seems to be fairly clever."

Miles said, "Well, she was dating Darren, after all. I don't think anyone but another reader would have been a good match for him."

"Exactly. Anyway, I think she'll fully support my plan to read *House of Mirth*. And we'll have the chance to speak with her about Darren," said Myrtle.

Miles shook his head. "There's no way she'll be there, Myrtle. Darren *just* died. She's probably just found out about it from Red. Tomorrow morning she may want nothing more than staying in bed all day with the covers pulled over her head."

Miles had sounded far too wistful at that last bit. She'd have to do everything in her considerable power to keep him distracted. "Ordinarily, I'd agree with you. But you know how Tippy is. She thinks the best way to handle grief is distraction. I bet you anything Tippy will go right over to Pansy's house and trot her directly over to the library for our meeting."

The waitress came by the table and glanced at Miles's untouched salad. "Can I box that up for you, hon?"

Miles winced and shook his head rapidly. "I'm all done."

Myrtle said, "For heaven's sake, Miles! Box it up and eat it for supper. You'll be hungry again eventually."

Miles shook his head stubbornly and Myrtle sighed. She asked the waitress, "Do you mind boxing it? I may eat it for supper, myself."

As the waitress whisked it away, Myrtle said, "Here. I saved you some French fries." Miles shook his head again and Myrtle pushed the plate at him. "Have one. Sometimes greasy food is better."

Miles could tell that Myrtle wasn't going to be dissuaded. He reluctantly put a fry in his mouth. It sat well enough, however, that he ended up eating the rest of them.

Myrtle gave the empty plate a look of satisfaction. "Healthy food isn't all it's cracked up to be. Sometimes a little good old-fashioned comfort food is better."

They paid their bills and headed back to Miles's car. Miles started up the engine. "How about if I drop you back home, Myrtle? I think I may take a nap."

Myrtle didn't think much of that plan. Miles might have a maudlin tendency to dwell on things. "Actually, I need your help. Let's go to the grocery store and I'll pick up a few things for book club tomorrow."

Miles gave her a startled look. "You're not cooking, are you?"

"The expression on your face, Miles! Why *shouldn't* I cook? I want everyone to enjoy being at the library tomorrow."

"Precisely." Miles's voice was dry.

"I have some really wonderful old recipes for hors d'oeuvres that the rest of the ladies are sure to love."

Miles said pointedly, "Do you have the recipes with you? Sometimes you don't remember the ingredients when we're shopping. It forces you to make creative substitutions."

"People go to *school* to learn how to cook. *We* went to school to learn how to cook. It's an art . . . a creative endeavor. Substituting is the way to make something average truly great."

Miles appeared doubtful at this. "What are you planning on bringing?"

"A couple of favorites from the 1970s."

Miles flinched. "I don't recall the 70s being especially well-known for its culinary contributions."

"You're clearly forgetting olive balls."

Miles said fervently, "Clearly, I am."

"They were very good and very easy. They had olives and cheese and whatnot."

It was the whatnot Miles was worried about.

Myrtle said, "And I really think I should make something for poor Orabelle."

Miles muttered something that sounded very much like *she doesn't deserve that.*

Myrtle gave him a sharp look and continued, "Perhaps a casserole of some sort. One filled with the comfort foods we were just talking about."

Miles looked alarmed. "A French fry casserole?"

"Don't be silly, Miles. Of course not. No, this would be a *tater tot* casserole. That's much fancier than French fries, but has the same tummy-filling comfort."

"And you remember the ingredients?"

Myrtle said, "Certainly. I've made it many, many times. Red will remember."

"So the last time you made it, Red was still a kid?" Miles now looked even more alarmed. Red was in his late-forties.

"Making it will be muscle-memory. It will all come right back to me. It has cream-of-something soup in it and some vegetables." Myrtle didn't sound too certain about the pesky particulars.

In a few minutes, they were at the grocery store. Miles morosely pushed the cart while Myrtle thoughtfully perused the shelves, trying to remember the suddenly elusive ingredients of the tater tot casserole.

"Well, we know it has tater tots in it," said Miles dryly.

"We do. Good point, Miles. Let's start with what we know and then the rest of the ingredients might naturally fall into place." They walked to the other end of the store and got a bag of the frozen grated potatoes.

Myrtle became distracted in the frozen food section and ended up with ice cream and frozen waffles.

"Surely those aren't going in." Miles frowned at the items as Myrtle threw them in the cart.

"Don't be absurd. Of course, they won't. But now I need to find something for me to snack on. It occurs to me that I don't have much in my house right now. Besides, both these things are on sale."

There were, apparently, many things on sale at the store. Miles watched glumly as the groceries piled up in Myrtle's cart. "Have you figured out what else might be in the recipe?"

"Olives," muttered Myrtle as she threw in a box of cereal.

"In the tater tot casserole?" Miles's voice was scandalized.

"No, no, in the olive cheese balls. I have *two* recipes, remember?"

Miles was trying hard not to.

Myrtle ended up getting olives and tater tots and cream of mushroom soup. She felt sure she likely had the other ingredients at her house. Besides, the cart was getting quite full with sale items and she wanted to make sure her bank account was able to handle the hit.

After checking out, Miles pushed the cart full of bags to his car. Myrtle grumbled, "That was an excessive amount to pay for groceries. Those things were all allegedly on sale."

"I don't think it's the price of the individual items. I think it's the *collective* price as a whole."

"Spoken like a true CPA." Myrtle plopped down in the front seat and scowled out the window.

"Engineer," said Miles coldly.

"Whatever. This will curtail my spending for the rest of the week until my retirement check comes in. That's so bothersome."

"Were you planning on spending money? That sounds rather unlike you."

"I suppose not. But I might have wanted to return to the grocery store for a few items. I didn't have my list with me so I just shopped the sale. Now I'm not altogether sure if the things I purchased can be assembled into any sort of a meal or not." Myrtle frowned.

Miles thought back over the items in the cart. "Well, I know you can make meals out of cereal. You did purchase a box of cereal."

"But I'm not at all sure I have milk. This is all very vexing! Miles, you're so reasonable . . . you should have stopped me."

"You're a force of nature, Myrtle. Unstoppable. You were very focused on buying things on sale."

Myrtle said, "Which *seems* fiscally conservative until you realize you don't actually have anything to eat. I recall putting a good deal of laundry soap in the cart."

"It was buy one, get one free, I believe." Miles pulled into Myrtle's driveway.

Myrtle mused for a moment. "Hm. Perhaps it would be a good time to see more of my family. And friends." She gave Miles a sideways glance.

Miles sighed. "You know you're welcome to eat over at my house. But you usually don't like the offerings there."

"That's only because you have a very odd taste in food. There's always a lot of watercress at your house. And cucumber. And blue cheese-stuffed-olives."

"You just *bought* olives. Clearly, you like them," pointed out Miles reasonably.

"Not as an entire meal."

Miles frowned. "Have I eaten olives as an entire meal?" He shook his head. "Anyway, I have a simple solution for this. You'll find your grocery list here at the house. We'll head back to the store with your receipt and we'll return items you don't want. You'll get the things you need to make meals for the next week and you'll have food until your check comes."

Myrtle said, "That's no good. You know who works at the customer service counter."

"Do I?"

"That Tracy Thudmore. She's ghastly and she has a big mouth." Myrtle made a face.

Miles said mildly, "I'm not sure returning unwanted food would constitute a scandal, Myrtle."

"Of course it would. We're in Bradley. Tracy would tell everyone that I lost my mind and bought a cart full of groceries and returned nearly every bit of it. Then the next thing I know, Red will stick me in Greener Pastures Retirement Home and I'll be stuck eating their disgusting food. You'll come visit me and we'll be enduring canned pears with mayonnaise and grated cheese." Myrtle shuddered.

"Or she'll say you're a smart shopper who realized too late that she didn't shop around her weekly menus."

Myrtle said, "*Or* she'll say that I'm too broke to take home random groceries. No, Miles, the damage has been done. I'll simply snack on whatever I purchased and then camp out at your place and Red's for meals. I suppose I can get used to cucumber and olives."

"Great," said Miles without enthusiasm. He followed her in, helping to carry groceries. "Do you need a hand putting this stuff away?"

"Nope. I'm all good." She peered at him through narrowed eyes. "But now I think we should watch *Tomorrow's Promise* together."

Miles looked at her suspiciously. "Are you trying to keep me here under false pretenses?"

"Since when has our soap opera constituted false pretenses? Besides, we can sit around and snack on chips. I appear to have lots of chips."

Miles said, "You're not worried about me, are you?"

"Me? Of course not. After all, at our age, we're accustomed to losing friends." Regardless of the questionable truth of that statement, Myrtle suspected Miles could still use a diversion.

"We're not *quite* the same age," said Miles stiffly.

"But we're both seniors. We're in the same age *category*. And *Tomorrow's Promise* is going to be especially good today. We'll get to find out who poisoned Antonia and who's the father of Gretchen's baby."

Miles shook his head. "I just don't know. I'm feeling a little restless. I'm not sure I can sit down and even pay attention to a TV set."

Myrtle unloaded a few more of the bags and thought this through. She brightened. "I know exactly what we should do. We should visit Wanda." Wanda was a friend of Myrtle's, a cousin of Miles's, and was a psychic to boot.

Miles groaned. "I'm pretty sure I'm not up to a visit with Wanda today."

"You know how helpful she is. She has a completely different perspective on things."

"I'll agree with that." Miles watched glumly as Myrtle put away a can of French-fried onions. "At least, I'll agree on the 'completely different perspective' part."

Myrtle said, "It's important to hear her thoughts at the very beginning of an investigation. Otherwise, we waste time. It's also likely time for us to check in with her and see how she's doing."

Miles sighed. "That's the part that's so difficult. She's always struggling."

"Not true. She gave up smoking and that's really helped her health."

Miles said, "Except she still coughs and her voice is completely ruined."

"She's given away all the piles of junk that her brother had collected in the shack."

"Except Crazy Dan keeps bringing in more," said Miles.

"And Sloan has improved her lifestyle by giving Wanda a well-deserved raise for her column."

"It's a horoscope, not a column," pointed out Miles.

"The way Wanda writes it, it *is* a column." Myrtle put away the last of the groceries and headed for her front door.

Miles sighed. "Just hop in the car and I'll be there in a minute. I need to run home. I'll need to grab cash and some hand sanitizer."

Myrtle knew better than to try to argue. Whenever they saw Wanda, Miles was always exceptionally paranoid about touching things without using hand sanitizer. And he never left Wanda without putting a bit of cash into her hand.

Chapter Four

The old rural route highway was a museum of small businesses from the past. There was an ancient motel that still had a sign out front advertising color TVs in the rooms. There was a diner that never seemed to have any customers. There were church billboards scattered along the way that started with the affirming "Jesus Loves You" before becoming rapidly more dire (culminating with "Choose the Bread of Life or You Are Toast!") And then, finally, there was the hubcap-covered shack where Wanda resided with her brother Crazy Dan. They had a sign, as well: it advertised live bait, boiled peanuts, and fortunes from Wanda.

Miles parked the car in the middle of the red clay, grassless yard. The borders of the property were marked by wheel-less cars atop cement blocks. The curtains fluttered inside the shack.

Myrtle frowned. "Looks like Crazy Dan is home."

"Wonderful," said Miles with a groan. "Did you spot him through a window?"

"No, but Wanda never has to look out to know we're here. She always knows we're coming." Myrtle climbed out of the car.

Miles pressed his lips in a thin line. He was never fond of hearing about Wanda's gifts.

Myrtle rapped on one of the hubcaps on the house with her cane and a wild-looking man opened the door. "It's *you*," he barked as if Myrtle and Miles visited half a dozen times a day.

"Delighted to see you, too, Dan," said Myrtle, sweeping past him into the dimly-lit home. She was glad to see that in the war between Crazy Dan's hoarding and Wanda's cleaning, Wanda currently appeared to have the upper-hand. "Is Wanda home?"

"A-course she is. Knew you wuz comin' didn't she?" He picked up a golf club from a cluttered corner and knit his bushy eyebrows as he peered around. "Seen my gawf balls?"

Myrtle shook her head and Miles cleared his throat and reached under the coffee table. That was a feat in itself because the coffee table was partially obscured by some stacks of Dan's things. "Here's one."

Dan beamed at the golf ball and snatched it out of Miles's hand. "Good. Got to practice my swing."

Myrtle said sternly, "Before you head out, where *is* Wanda?"

He scowled at her. "Picking herbs out back. Be right in." And with that, he popped out of the house with the golf club and ball, looking rather like a sportive oversized troll.

Miles immediately pulled the bottle of hand sanitizer out of the pocket of his khakis and squirted a generous portion into his hands.

"You must go through that stuff like crazy," said Myrtle.

"I buy it in bulk," said Miles, replacing the bottle into his pocket.

Wanda hurried in through the back door, looking tired but happy. She had a little plastic pot with an herb in it and proffered it to Myrtle. "Thought you might want to spice up some of yer cookin.'"

Myrtle leaned over and drew in a deep breath. "Basil?"

Wanda beamed at her, revealing missing teeth in the process.

Myrtle took the basil and sat with it in her lap as if it were a precocious infant. "Thank you, Wanda. Garden club will be most impressed that I'm branching out into herbs."

Miles glanced unhappily around the room for a place to sit. He finally gingerly perched on a rather rickety chair that had seen better days. He absently patted the pocket that held his hand sanitizer as if it comforted him.

Wanda looked at them shrewdly. "Yer wonderin' about that murder."

"You know about that?" asked Miles, startled.

"Of *course* she does, Miles. For heaven's sake, how are you always surprised at Wanda's abilities?" Myrtle gave him an exasperated look.

Wanda, however, gave him a sympathetic smile. "Y'all was friends."

Miles gave a quick swallow. "We were."

"He's in a better place," said Wanda with conviction.

Myrtle had always thought this a rather comfortless platitude with which to offer the grieving. But the way Wanda used it, it sounded as if she knew something they didn't.

Myrtle said, "Regardless, it wasn't his time to go."

"Reckon somebody thought differently," said Wanda.

"Do you know whom that somebody might be?" asked Myrtle.

Wanda gave her a sad look. "The sight just don't work that way. Wish it did."

Myrtle nodded briskly. "I remember. I guess I keep asking because I'd like the answer to be different or I hope things have somehow changed. How about this: do you have any insights about the murder? Any recommendations about anyone we should speak with or what sorts of questions we should ask?"

"Yer in danger," said Wanda. "Shouldn't be askin' questions."

"Yes, yes, I know all about that. My advanced years make me fearless, Wanda. No one will say 'what a pity! Myrtle died so very young!' Besides, I always find a way to get out of my jams."

Wanda sighed and said, "Reckon you should talk to that lawyer."

Miles scowled. "Naturally there's a lawyer involved in this murder."

"I'm guessing you're speaking of Liam Hudson? Even in a town the size of Bradley, there's more than one," said Myrtle.

"Too many lawyers," muttered Miles.

Wanda said, "Reckon it's Liam." She suddenly looked tired and turned back to Myrtle. "You been gardenin' lately?"

"Not as much as you have, apparently. It's been rather discouraging. My next-door neighbor, Erma, has callous disregard for the weeds she's allowing to come traipsing over to my property."

Wanda gave her an intent look. "Them weeds is bad."

"Indeed, they are."

Wanda tilted her head slightly. "Maybe you should do somethin' about 'em."

Myrtle said, "Well, ordinarily I'd say that would be fighting a losing battle, but I suppose I could give it a try. Especially since *you're* the one telling me to." She paused. "Any other words of wisdom?"

Miles muttered something about lawyers and weeds under his breath.

Wanda said, "Elaine's got a new hobby."

Myrtle and Miles both sighed. Elaine's hobbies never seemed to go very well and sometimes they went very poorly indeed.

"What is it this time?" asked Myrtle.

"Bakin'," said Wanda.

Myrtle said, "Oh, thank heavens. She can cook." She frowned. "Hm. Wonder if that's why Red was looking pudgy earlier today. At any rate, that bodes well for my week of needing to supplement what I have at my house."

Wanda nodded and narrowed her eyes. "Be careful."

"Of course I will," said Myrtle briskly.

Miles rolled his eyes.

"Well, I think we'll go ahead and get out of your hair now. I need to speak to Sloan in a bit about my article for the paper. Do you want me to hand him any of your horoscopes?"

Wanda shook her head. "Ain't got any yet. Nuthin's come to me."

"That's all right. You can just call me when you have something. Your phone is still working, isn't it?" asked Myrtle.

Myrtle could see Miles glancing around the shack for signs of working electricity. It was never that the phone wasn't working: it was that it couldn't be charged when the electricity had been turned off for lack of payment.

"Yep, we're in good shape. With that extra money Sloan done give me."

"He hasn't *given* you anything, Wanda, you've *earned* it. He has so many more subscribers to the paper now that you're writing for it. The least he could do is share some of that income with the person responsible." Myrtle stood up and grabbed her cane to make sure she could navigate out of the dim house well. Miles stood up, breathing a sigh of relief.

They said their goodbyes as Miles quietly pressed some cash into Wanda's hand. Then they headed to Miles's car. Crazy Dan was searching for his golf ball in what appeared to be a large patch of poison oak that had somehow managed to grow from the red clay of the soil. Wanda waved to them as they drove away.

Myrtle gazed thoughtfully out the window as Miles drove toward town. He glanced over at her. "Do you think we found out anything helpful?"

"Yes, indeed. We found that Wanda is doing better. The house, although cluttered, wasn't *nearly* as bad as we've seen it in the past."

"But besides that. The case." Miles carefully watched the road as if deer, raccoons, rabbits, and other woodland creatures might leap from the heavy vegetation on the sides of the road at any moment.

"Well, there's that lawyer lead. I didn't know anything about that. I suppose we'll need to speak with Pansy about him at the book club meeting tomorrow. And apparently, I need to take care of my weed problem for some reason. The thing I'm *most* excited about, though, is Elaine's new hobby. This might end up being a wonderful week, after all."

The rest of the ride back, Myrtle kept up cheery commentary from the passenger seat. She was glad to see that Miles wasn't apparently brooding over Darren anymore. Maybe taking an active role in figuring out what happened to him would fix it. After all, he was her sidekick.

"Want to come inside?" asked Myrtle. "If you're not restless anymore, we can watch our show."

Miles shook his head. "No, thanks. Actually, I feel pretty exhausted. I'm going to eat something, read my book, and crawl in the bed early."

"Sounds good. See you tomorrow. Why don't we get started early-ish? We can bring my casserole over to Orabelle's house. Maybe Tripp will be there."

Miles balked. "Do we *want* to disturb a grieving sister early in the day with a casserole?" His tone suggested it was a ghastly idea.

"Disturb? No, we're *helping*. That's what we do in a small town when someone dies . . . we heap food on them. Goodness, Miles, you'd think you'd just moved over from Atlanta yesterday."

Miles returned home and Myrtle bustled into her house and straight to the kitchen. She had a feeling that Pasha, the feral cat who'd taken up with her, might be hanging around and wanting a can of food. She opened the kitchen window and sure enough, the black cat bounded inside.

"Brilliant Pasha," said Myrtle, crooning to the cat. She carefully checked to make sure the aforementioned brilliant feline wasn't carrying a living, half-dead, or deceased rodent in her mouth as sometimes happened. Satisfied this wasn't the case, she opened a can of tuna and dumped it onto a paper plate.

Pasha gave her an approving look through half-closed eyes and made short work of the tuna as Myrtle picked up the phone to call Sloan Jones, her editor at the local paper. Myrtle wrote a helpful hints column which had originally been Red's idea to keep her busy. But she also pressured Sloan, a former English student of hers from back in the day, to let her write regular articles for the paper, much to Red's dismay.

Sloan had apparently already made it to the pub that was in walking distance of the newspaper office when she called.

"Miz Myrtle!" he gasped when he heard her voice on the other end of the line. He immediately reverted to being in high school . . . and in trouble for late homework.

"Hi Sloan," said Myrtle briskly. She paused. "It's rather noisy where you are, isn't it?"

Sloan apparently quickly stepped outside of the pub and into the quiet street outside. "Um, just a band of people going by."

"A band of rather raucous people."

"Yes. Yes, they were. But they're gone now." Sloan quickly added, "What can I help you with?"

"It's more a question of what *I* can help *you* with, Sloan. I'm going to write an article for you tonight and wanted to see if you can stick it in the paper tomorrow."

Sloan's voice now sounded anxious. "Miz Myrtle, I just put the paper to bed. It's all set for printing."

Myrtle didn't say anything, just waited.

Sloan didn't like that tactic. "Uh, I suppose I could stick a piece on the back page. I'd just have to reduce one of the ads there a little and make a few other changes."

"That would work if it were a helpful hints column. But it decidedly won't work for a front-page investigative story."

"And that's what you have?" Sloan sounded a bit squeaky.

"Yes, indeed."

"Did someone die? I must have missed that."

Myrtle had found that Sloan frequently got caught up in the most-local of the local stories to the detriment of proper journalism. He paid far too much attention to Maisy Wellborn's prize-winning tomatoes and far less-attention to what he considered "stressful articles": the sad state of the bridge stretching over the lake, for instance. And various crime stories of great regional importance.

"Yes, indeed. Darren Powell died this morning."

Sloan sounded relieved, as if finding a workable solution for his problem. "Oh, well, I'm very sorry to hear that. Amazing that I didn't get that gossip today. I can put an obituary in, no problem." He paused and then fearfully asked, "You did say something about an investigative story, though."

"Darren was murdered."

Sloan heaved a huge sigh. "Oh, no." Then he quickly added, "But hey . . . "

"Sloan, I don't want to hear a thing come out of your mouth right now. I know precisely what you're about to say: 'Miz Myrtle, Red will have my hide if you cover that story.'"

Sloan sighed again. Myrtle had the feeling he might be looking longingly at the bar he'd just vacated. "All right. Just . . . don't get into any trouble, okay? I guess I can print the paper a little later tonight, but I can't hold it for long."

Myrtle said briskly, "I'll have it all ready for you in thirty minutes, perfectly edited."

She hung up and got right to work. Sure enough, thirty minutes later she emailed the article over to Sloan. Then she settled down to relax for a while before turning in.

Pasha had decided to hang around for a while. She curled up on the sofa in a ball and kept an eye on Myrtle as she finally finished the crossword from that morning. She decided she was under no obligation to wait for Miles to watch the next exciting episode of *Tomorrow's Promise*. As expected, it was quite a thrilling installment.

Perhaps it had been a little *too* thrilling. Antonia's poisoner had proven a shock as well as the big reveal over the father of Gretchen's baby. That, plus the excitement of the day, made it difficult for Myrtle to wind down.

"Are you sure you want to stay overnight?" asked Myrtle doubtfully as she stared at Pasha.

Pasha watched her with one eye open.

"I'll keep a window open for you in case you want to leave. We don't usually have sleepovers."

Pasha yawned as if to say that a sleepover suited her fine right then.

"All right then." Myrtle opened the kitchen window and then got ready for bed.

Two hours later, she stared up at the crack on her bedroom ceiling that always reminded her of a rabbit. She sighed and got out of bed.

She was astonished to see Pasha was still there. Pasha, on the other hand, didn't seem astonished at all to see her as if she'd known Myrtle wasn't down for the night. They were both nocturnal animals.

Myrtle pulled a robe and her slippers out of her closet. Pasha jumped quietly down and padded after her.

"Let's go for a nice stroll. The night air will do us good." Myrtle opened the front door and Pasha bounded out as Myrtle followed her.

Pasha headed for the sidewalk and took a right, looking expectantly behind her.

"Excellent idea," murmured Myrtle. "Miles might be up, no matter what he said. We'll look to see if his lights are on. If he's up, he might want company. Or, perhaps, to continue playing chess."

But when they reached Miles's house, it seemed rather dim at first glance. Myrtle peered toward the back of the house and finally did see light.

Chapter Five

"**N**ow, does that look like a nightlight? Or a regular light?" asked Myrtle, glancing down at the black cat. Pasha padded up the walkway to Miles's front door, then looked meaningfully behind her at Myrtle.

Myrtle followed and rang the doorbell.

Miles answered the door wearing pajamas and a robe and appearing a bit grouchy. He was, however, clearly awake. He held the door open for Myrtle and grunted as Pasha entered behind her.

"Pasha and I are spending some time together," said Myrtle by way of explanation. "Since you were up, we thought we'd include you in our little visit."

Miles said coldly, "I hadn't fully committed to being awake yet. I was still mulling over whether I wanted to try to go to sleep again." He glared at Pasha, as if it were all her fault.

Myrtle bustled by him toward his kitchen. Pasha's eyes danced as she looked at Miles and then padded after Myrtle.

"You wouldn't fall back asleep again. Trust me, I'm an expert on all things related to insomnia. You'd simply burn through a couple of restless hours tossing and turning. No, it's far better to go ahead and give up and get up. Maybe you can take a little nap later, after we dispense the casserole."

Miles muttered something about "dispensing" that Myrtle didn't quite catch.

"Don't be so cranky, Miles. Here, I'll make coffee and toast." She briskly set to making them as Pasha leapt up into a kitchen chair and watched.

The doorbell rang and they both froze.

"Who on earth could *that* be?" Myrtle frowned.

Miles walked cautiously to the front door to find out. He peeked outside and spun around. "Erma!" he hissed.

Myrtle made frantic waving motions to indicate Erma should stay safely on the other side of the door. "No! Pretend we're not here."

"She clearly saw you come in."

"I'm not ready to deal with Erma yet today, Miles. She'll give up in a minute."

But Erma apparently had no plans of giving up. She knocked. She rang the bell. She called their names. Miles finally, reluctantly, opened the door.

"There you are!" Erma beamed at them, her large, rodent-like teeth gleaming. "What on earth took you so long to answer the door?"

Myrtle said in a surly voice, "I turned the fan on because I burned the toast. We couldn't hear over it."

Erma gave her donkey, hee-hawing laugh. "Burned the toast! I believe it. So we're having a pajama party, are we?" She glanced in delight at Myrtle in her long robe and slippers, Miles in his plaid pajamas and navy-blue robe with matching slippers, and then at her own rather peculiar and wildly-printed pajama set. Erma looked like some sort of ghastly Auntie Mame.

"There's something you should know, Erma," said Myrtle coldly. "We're not the only two visitors here."

Erma's nose started twitching. Her eyes began watering. She gasped. "That cat's in here?"

Myrtle nodded. "She's the guest of honor here, actually. It was practically Pasha's idea to come to Miles's house in the first place. And she never gets to come."

Miles, who wasn't ordinarily Pasha's greatest fan, gave the cat a grateful look. Erma's cat allergy was fairly virulent.

"I never get to come either," said Erma, still in that gasping voice. "Thought I'd check in for once when I couldn't sleep."

"Here, I'll give you some things to take home with you." The emphasis seemed to be on *home*. Myrtle rooted around in the cabinet and pulled out a chipped mug. She filled it with coffee.

"Cream, please," gasped Erma. She sneezed. "And sugar."

Myrtle doctored the coffee, grabbed a piece of cold, over-cooked toast and proffered them to Erma.

Erma took them and wheezed her way back out of the house.

Myrtle locked the door behind her.

Miles gave her an admiring look. "Well done."

"It was all due to darling Pasha. You should really stop giving her short shrift, Miles. She's positively brilliant. I'm convinced she knew exactly what she was doing and was protecting us from Erma."

Pasha, still at the kitchen table, gave them a knowing look and began contentedly licking her paws.

"She deserves some sort of treat," said Miles fervently.

Myrtle said, "She's had some tuna at my house, but she'd probably eat more."

"I don't have tuna, but I have canned salmon."

And so Pasha commenced to eating a salmon feast.

Myrtle poured them both some coffee and put the toast on a plate.

Miles looked at the dark, dry pieces of toast and pulled out butter and jam. They settled at the table.

"In a way," said Miles thoughtfully, "I almost feel sorry for Erma."

"No one can feel sorry for Erma. It's utterly impossible."

"I do, though. She feels left out. She lives right next door and never gets to participate when we're having gatherings in the middle of the night," said Miles.

Myrtle said, "She does it all to herself. If she'd stayed a moment longer, she'd have been regaling us with her latest grotesque health issue. Besides, the fact that she hasn't participated in our gatherings means she's *sleeping*. Can you imagine? I can't picture falling asleep and then not remembering the next eight hours. That would be a gift. Certainly nothing to feel sorry about."

"I suppose."

Myrtle decided Miles was looking a bit mopey again. "Tell you what. Why don't we play chess and talk?"

"You don't like playing chess." Miles looked morosely at his toast, which was apparently not sufficiently improved by the slathered jam.

"I don't think I said that. It's simply not my most favorite, that's all."

Miles pushed his plate away from him and Pasha stared at it with interest. "You're wanting to talk about the murder."

Myrtle took his plate, dumped the toast, and put the plate in the dishwasher. "Let's put it this way, Miles. If you look at the murder through a lens, it might be a little easier on you. You need some distance. Talking it over from a different perspective will help you out."

Miles trudged behind her into the living room and sat in front of the chess board. Pasha followed and leapt into Myrtle's lap. "What a little love," crooned Myrtle to the feral cat.

"She's had a very good night," said Miles, a bit more cynically. "Tuna *and* salmon. It must be a red-letter day for Pasha."

Myrtle gestured to the chess board. "I believe it's your move."

Miles frowned. "Is it? I remember it being yours."

"I'm feeling generous."

Miles studied the board and took Myrtle's pawn.

Myrtle glanced over the board and took Miles's other bishop.

Miles groaned.

"I may feel badly for you, Miles, but that doesn't mean I don't want to win the game." Myrtle gave him a reproving look.

Miles said darkly, "Why do I have the feeling you're much better at chess than you make out?"

Myrtle ignored this. "How about if you tell me more about Darren? And about his discovery in the attic."

Miles was still focused on the chess board, trying to figure out a better next move than his last one had been. "I don't know anything about that, as you're aware. You were here with me."

"No, no, I don't mean *that* one. I mean the *first* discovery in the attic. The one that made him money."

Miles sat back thoughtfully in his chair. "Well, there's not very much to tell. He had a bunch of things in his attic and he decided to clear it out."

"Were these *his* things in the attic? Or was the attic still full of a previous owner's things?"

Miles said, "No, these were his. But he hadn't actually gone through them. There had been some deaths in the past years in his family and he'd ended up with a lot of boxes and bags in the process. He didn't have time to deal with them because he was still working so he'd put them up in the attic to handle later. They stayed up there until he finally got around to dealing with them."

Myrtle said, "And Orabelle didn't get any of these things? That seems rather odd."

"My understanding is that it was his wife's family. Once she passed away, Darren was really the only one left, even though he was related by marriage." Miles put his hand on his knight and then moved it away again rapidly. "At the time, it seemed more of a hassle than anything else."

"Until he discovered the painting." Myrtle sighed when she saw Miles release the knight.

Miles looked at her sharply and then studied the chess board again. He absently said, "Yes. When he discovered the painting, he realized it might be worth something."

"And it ended up being a Degas or a Van Gogh or something."

Miles frowned at her. "No. Darren didn't suddenly become a multi-millionaire overnight. But it was an 'important' find. That's what the experts said. I can't remember the name of the artist. But the painting was worth several hundred thousand dollars."

Miles tentatively placed his hand on his rook and Myrtle's eyes grew wide. He drew his hand back as if the chess piece had burned him.

Miles said irritably, "I can't believe you don't remember all this. It happened just a year or so ago and it was in the *Bradley Bugle*."

"Yes, but to me it was lumped in with all the rest of Sloan's 'feel-good' stories. You know: the prize-winning apple pie, the fisherman with the tremendous catch. The valuable painting in the attic." Myrtle shrugged. Then her eyes narrowed. "So the paper printed how much the painting was worth?"

"Not just what it was worth. What it actually drew at an auction."

Myrtle considered this. "So everyone knew. Including his family."

"Well, sure." Miles put his hand on another pawn and moved it without looking at Myrtle this time. "Are you saying his family might have wanted to do him in for financial reasons?"

"I'm only saying it might be a motive. And I saw a pair of sunglasses in Darren's yard that I'm sure couldn't have been his.

They certainly didn't look like Orabelle's either, although she was very interested in them." Myrtle took Miles's bishop.

Miles groaned. "Maybe we should play at another time. I don't seem to have my mind totally focused."

Myrtle rubbed Pasha. "That's fine. Soon the paper will arrive and we can work on the puzzles." She frowned. "I could go ahead and make my casserole for Orabelle. That does need to be done."

Miles sighed. "I wish you'd just let it go, Myrtle. Maybe we could just bring her some bagels and cream cheese."

Myrtle stared at him. "Bagels and cream cheese? As comfort food after a family member's demise? For heaven's sake, Miles. I can promise you that's not a tradition in Bradley. Plus, there's the fact that I'm out of funds until my check comes."

"Right, I'd forgotten about that. All right, then, I guess make your casserole. Don't you want breakfast, as well? Not just toast?"

Myrtle shifted slightly in her chair and Pasha took the hint and gracefully jumped to the floor. Myrtle stood up. "No, I don't think so. My plan is to go over and sample some of these baked goods of Elaine's. Jack's such an early riser that it shouldn't be too long. Plus, I want to check the paper and make sure Sloan did justice to my story yesterday."

"He agreed to let you write a story on Darren's death?" Miles raised his eyebrows.

"It only took a little pushing."

Miles said, "I predict you'll have a very interesting breakfast at Red's house."

"If he knows what's good for him, he won't say a thing." Myrtle sniffed.

Chapter Six

As Myrtle walked back a few minutes later, she peered carefully at Red and Elaine's house but didn't see any lights on. She unlocked her door and walked in, holding the door open for Pasha. The feral cat, however, decided to go off on her own adventure and bounded away. At least she had a full stomach.

Myrtle set to preparing the casserole. She pulled out a battered cookbook from the 1970s and studied a spattered page. "For heaven's sake," she muttered. She'd have sworn the casserole didn't have green beans in it. Myrtle peered in her pantry. There wasn't a can of green beans to be found.

She sighed and pawed through the cans to find an appropriate substitute. Finally, she frowned at a couple of cans of asparagus that were hiding in the very back. Luckily, they appeared to still be a couple of months away from expiring so it was good to use them up. Besides, they were of about the same size and texture as green beans. And the same color, too.

Myrtle checked back with the recipe again, which somehow seemed completely different from what she'd remembered. The casserole had ground beef in it and she certainly didn't recall it being a meaty casserole. She dubiously opened her freezer to find no ground beef whatsoever. There was frozen chicken, though. At least she had the cream of mushroom soup. She hadn't realized she was out of Worcestershire sauce, but she had light soy sauce which she carefully mixed in. The cheese present-ed another problem until Myrtle realized she had grated Parme-san cheese in a can in the back of her fridge.

The longest part of the compilation process was defrosting the frozen chicken. For some reason, the chicken simply refused to defrost. She knew she'd set the correct defrosting function on the microwave, yet the ends were cooking and the middle was completely icy.

Myrtle checked the recipe again. "Well, if the chicken is cooking at 375 degrees, it certainly won't be frozen by the time it's all finished."

So Myrtle mixed everything together and then put the tater tot potatoes on the top. She looked at it in satisfaction and popped it into the oven. It needed to cook for 40 minutes, which would give Myrtle plenty of time to check the newspaper story and then see if there were signs of life over at Elaine and Red's house.

The newspaper article was there on the front page. Sloan had somehow found a picture of Darren and it accompanied the story. Satisfied, Myrtle put the paper on her coffee table. Spot-ting lights on at her son's house, she traipsed across the street.

Red opened the door and groaned when he saw his mother there. He appeared to be in the process of getting ready for the day with his uniform on, but his top was only half-buttoned. He held Jack, who looked grouchy until he spotted his beloved Nana. Then he gave Myrtle a big smile.

"See, I'm already having a beneficial effect on the household," said Myrtle briskly.

"That's sorely needed. Here, you sit down on the sofa and I'll put Jack down next to you with some of his trucks. Then maybe I can actually get ready for my day."

A few seconds later, Jack was busily driving his trucks over Myrtle's arm.

"Where's Elaine?" asked Myrtle.

Red rubbed his face as if trying to wake up. "In the kitchen. Baking." He lowered his voice. "It's the new hobby." He gave Myrtle a meaningful look. They had both seen a lot of hobbies come and go.

"But a good one. Elaine is an excellent cook." Jack was now trying to play "crash" with the trucks, so Myrtle picked one up and gave him a target.

"Agreed. But the problem this time is my waistline." Red gave his stomach a regretful look.

Myrtle said, "That's why this visit of mine is again beneficial. I need to eat. You need to unload baked goods. It's the perfect solution."

Red put his hands on his hips. "Is that why you're here? To eat?"

"I appear to be short on funds until the end of the week," said Myrtle with dignity.

"I could have sworn I saw Miles helping unload your car yesterday. It sure looked like a lot of groceries." Red was now beginning to look suspicious.

"It was. Unfortunately, however, I didn't go with a list. There was nothing really to make meals out of."

Red said, "That doesn't sound like you. Are you sure you're not here to squeeze information from me about this case?"

Myrtle glared at him. "Red Clover! Here is your elderly mother, admitting her poverty and all you can think about is that I might be trying to horn in on your case!"

Red held up his hands. "All right, all right. I'm just saying, usually you're a lot more fiscally-conservative until your check comes in."

"I *was* being fiscally-conservative. Every single thing I purchased was on sale. That's where I went wrong. I was led astray by buy-one-get-one free deals." She paused. "But how *is* your case going? I'm only asking because I'm concerned about you and how your life comes to a screeching halt every time you have something big to work on."

Red said, "It's going just fine, Mama. Just fine. Now, if you'll excuse me, I'll grab the paper, munch on a buttery biscuit, and finish getting ready so I can start hunting the guy down."

Myrtle shifted uncomfortably at the mention of the paper. She'd seen it on their front walk, of course, and decided to leave it where it lay.

"For heaven's sake, Red, why not finish getting ready first? You might scare people wandering outside in your current condition."

Red's eyebrows shot up. "I don't look *that* bad. What's in the paper that you don't want me to see?"

Myrtle frowned at him. "Absolutely nothing. I simply don't want the Clover family name to be so poorly represented."

Red strode to the door. "I have a sneaking suspicion."

Myrtle sighed and Jack, still busily crashing his truck into Myrtle's truck, looked up at her with concern. She beamed at him and said, "What a bright boy. Why don't you bring me a story?"

Jack carefully hopped down from the sofa and trotted off to find a book.

Red came back in, his face stormy. "I'm going to have to have a word with Sloan again."

"You're being ridiculous. All I'm doing is reporting. I'm not *making* the news."

"Yeah, but somehow you always end up getting yourself into a jam. I want you to leave this case alone, Mama. Don't you be asking questions and sticking your nose in where it doesn't belong. There's a dangerous individual out there." He crossed his arms and narrowed his eyes at her.

Myrtle snorted. "As if I have time to do anything. My day today is going to be monopolized by book club."

"Good. That should keep you out of trouble for a while." Red looked over at his son as Jack came running back in with a book and clambered back up the sofa to sit in Myrtle's lap. "And that story will keep you occupied, too."

Myrtle studied the cover. "Mr. Peebles is Sick." She frowned at Red. "Hardly great literature. We're going to have to work on your juvenile library collection."

Red chuckled. "It's Jack's favorite. Such a favorite that he likes to listen to it over and over again. In back-to-back fashion."

Myrtle summoned a brave smile and sniffed. "Clearly, you haven't the patience for such endeavors, but I do."

"And just be sure you don't mess up the virus's voice when that part comes up. It's got to sound really scary." Red's eyes were mischievous.

"You obviously don't recall that my storytelling skills are a tour de force." Jack snuggled up next to Myrtle and she put an arm around him. "And now it's time for me to read to my grandson."

Red took the hint and stomped off to finish getting ready.

Myrtle discovered that Mr. Peebles was indeed quite sick. The virus was dire and Myrtle apparently voiced it well because Jack was completely entranced. Naturally, Mr. Peebles was victorious at the end of the story, which Jack did indeed want to hear again.

By the third rendition of "Mr. Peebles is Sick," Myrtle was heartily sick herself . . . of Mr. Peebles. It seemed the sort of book her hypochondriac neighbor Erma would have on her bookshelf.

"We need to introduce you to *Mike Mulligan and His Steam Shovel*," muttered Myrtle to Jack. "Or perhaps *Babar*. And Dr. Seuss."

"Bye!" Red sang out as he happily left the house. Myrtle scowled after him. When Red came home later, she'd make sure her entire gnome collection was in her front yard. She'd call Dusty just as soon as she left the house. She gave a satisfied smile. Red hated looking across the street at her gnome army.

After a couple of minutes and just as Myrtle was wrapping up another retelling of the book, Elaine came in. She rolled her eyes. "I thought we'd made sure that book had been conveniently 'lost,'" she said apologetically.

Elaine scooped up Jack, who was still looking longingly at the story as if contemplating demanding yet another read of it. "Want some breakfast?" she asked with a smile.

Myrtle definitely did. Her stomach had been growling the whole time she was reading to Jack, despite the fact that the story focused on various illnesses. The aroma of freshly baked breads kept wafting from the kitchen. Myrtle had the feeling she was going to be able to easily eliminate a lot of Elaine's stock-piled baked goods.

A few minutes later, Myrtle was happily eating croissants with real butter. "This is your best hobby yet."

Elaine beamed at her as she gave Jack a plastic plate full of cut-up bits of bread and bananas. "Thanks! It's the tastiest, any-way. The only problem is that it makes so much."

Myrtle took a sip of water and said, "That may not be a problem at all. I was telling Red a few minutes ago that I find myself unexpectedly short on funds for the remainder of the week. I'll be happy to put a dent in your baking."

"Good. Red says he's getting heavier with all the extra food around, but I don't see it."

Myrtle figured Elaine must just be blissfully unaware. Or, possibly, in denial.

After Myrtle finished, she watched as Jack, now full, started carefully dropping little pieces of bread on the floor. He'd pick up a piece, look sideways at Myrtle, and then watch as it hit the floor.

"I should stop this, but for some reason, it's very entertaining," said Myrtle to Elaine as she gestured to the floor.

Elaine sighed and grabbed the bread from the floor. "He's clearly done. He's gotten into floor decorating lately. He apparently thinks it's some sort of new art form."

Myrtle said, "At least you have enough bread around here to waste. By the way, are you going to book club today?"

Elaine shook her head. "Jack doesn't have preschool today and I didn't read the book."

"I hardly think that matters. You could probably read the back cover and be able to discuss the story. You know how this book club's selections are."

"Just the same, I think I'll skip this one." She snapped her fingers. "But why don't you take some bread and pastries with you?"

Myrtle said, "I suppose I could. Although I'd already planned on bringing something else." She frowned suddenly. "What time is it?"

Elaine told her and Myrtle abruptly stood up. "I've got to run."

"Something wrong?" Elaine stuffed a couple of plastic bags full of baked goods into one of her hands.

Myrtle called behind her as she hurried to the door. "Only my casserole for Orabelle. It might be a little overcooked. See you later."

Myrtle was relieved to find there was no smoke in the house when she opened the door. She jerked open the oven door and was even more relieved to see there was no blackening of the casserole. However, it did seem a bit dry. Myrtle poked it with a fork. Then she opened her pantry door and discovered she had one more can of cream-of-something soup in the very back. She opened it and spread it carefully on top of the casserole like icing.

"There," she said, satisfied.

Myrtle decided to let the casserole cool for a while before sticking it in the fridge. Her next chore was to make some weed-killer since Wanda was so insistent about Erma's weeds. Myrtle disliked spraying pesticides in her yard, so made up her own concoction with a recipe from the internet she used before. It smelled a bit like a large Italian salad and made a lot more than she'd remembered it making. She poured it carefully into a large sprayer and decided she'd have Dusty take care of it when he was there. She also wanted him to take care of pulling her gnomes out, the sooner the better.

Glancing at the clock, Myrtle decided that if Dusty and his wife Puddin, Myrtle's housekeeper, weren't up already, they certainly should be. She picked up the phone.

After quite a few rings, a groggy Dusty picked up. "What's goin' on?" he howled into the phone.

"What's going on is morning. You should experience it, Dusty."

"It ain't mornin'! It's dark out there."

Myrtle said, "It's only dark because it's cloudy. For heaven's sake. Listen, I have some things for you to do today. As soon as possible."

"It ain't them gnomes again, is it?" asked Dusty in a sulky voice.

"It's the gnomes, yes. I need them all out in the front yard."

Dusty groaned.

"Pointed at Red's house, as usual," said Myrtle.

"Ain't enough room for all of 'em in the front! Some'll have to go in the back."

Myrtle said, "I'm sure you can find a way to put them *all* in the front yard. I want to make a real statement this time. And I have a new addition that I'd like to have front and center right in front of Red's house."

Dusty grunted. Then he asked curiously, "What's he done this time?"

"He's being pushy, as usual. Anyway, you don't have to worry about the reasons, just go ahead and do it. There's extra money for you for doing it."

"How much extra?" asked Dusty with interest.

"Extra. But you can't get it until next week because I'm short on funds this week."

He grunted again. "Guess I'll let Puddin know there ain't no reason to clean."

"There's *every* reason for her to clean. I paid her a couple of weeks ago and she left after five minutes saying her back was thrown and she needed time to recuperate. She owes me a cleaning." Myrtle's voice rose in irritation.

"Okay, okay," growled Dusty. He paused. "That it?"

"No, I also need you to spray weeds for me."

Dusty sighed. "Before or after I put them gnomes out?"

"Before, of course. I'll set the container outside my back door and you can spray to your heart's content. Be sure to get right up to the property line with Erma. You know how wily her weeds are. They'll sneak over into my yard with no provocation at all."

"Got it," said Dusty gloomily. "Better go." He rapidly hung up before Myrtle could assign him more tasks.

Myrtle hung up and looked at the casserole with her eyes narrowed. It looked somewhat like a sheet cake and this was bothering her for some reason. She opened her pantry and looked over the shelves. Apparently, one of the things on sale at the store had been French-fried onions. She opened the container and put them on top of the casserole and then appraised her work. It did look a lot more like a casserole this way. Satisfied, she covered the dish with tinfoil and put it in the fridge.

The doorbell rang and Myrtle opened the front door. Miles stood there, nose twitching like a rabbit.

Chapter Seven

"You've been cooking," he said in a somewhat accusatory tone.

"Of course I have. We had a whole discussion on this yesterday, Miles. You were with me when I bought ingredients. This is Orabelle's casserole. We're taking it to her now so we have plenty of time to do other things before book club."

"How did it turn out?"

Myrtle said, "Don't sound so suspicious. It turned out just fine. I tweaked the recipe to make it work with the things I had at home. And I even supplied a garnish for the top."

"A garnish?" Worried lines appeared across Miles's forehead.

"That's right. What's wrong with you? You'd think you'd never heard of a garnish before."

"So it's parsley? Basil? Something like that?" asked Miles.

Myrtle clapped her hands together which startled Miles. "Goodness! I forgot about Wanda's basil. I should put a bit of that on there, too."

She bustled into the kitchen and then to the back door. Opening the door, she found the pot of basil and carefully removed a leaf. Then she frowned at it. "Maybe I should bring it inside if Dusty is spraying weed killer. I can't trust him to know the difference between a weed and an herb, even if it *is* in a pot."

Miles watched from the kitchen door with apprehension as Myrtle uncovered the dish and put the basil inside.

"It smells wonderful," said Myrtle with satisfaction.

Miles peered around her at the casserole. "What's that stuff on top?"

"French-fried onions. They're my original garnish."

"Do French-fried onions qualify as a garnish?" Miles sounded doubtful.

"Certainly, they do! Everyone puts them on their Thanksgiving side dishes."

"Do they? I believe I've only seen them associated with green beans," said Miles.

Myrtle sniffed. "Clearly from some uncreative cooks."

"What's in the bags?" asked Miles, looking over at the counter.

"Elaine's baking," said Myrtle absently as she peered up at the wall clock. "I don't think it's too early to run this casserole by Orabelle's house. After all, she's a mail carrier. We'll need to catch up with her before she goes on her appointed rounds."

Miles made a face. "And we'll likely wake up her son. It's still very early, Myrtle."

"He has some explaining to do. It almost sounds like a Sherlock Holmes story. 'The Case of the Mysterious Sunglasses.'"

Miles looked into the bags of baked goods. "We don't know they're his sunglasses."

"But I strongly suspect they are."

Miles said, "These breads and muffins look very good." He gave her a hard look. "Why not use these instead? Maybe Orabelle and Tripp would rather have breakfast food right now than . . . that." He gestured to the casserole and gave a slight shudder.

"Yes, but I'm bringing most of the food to book club today. And I'd like to save a little bit for lunch. You'd like me to have lunch, wouldn't you?" Myrtle's voice was now gaining a tinge of irritation.

"I could host you at my house. Or I could treat you to Bo's Diner."

Myrtle's eyes narrowed. "How very generous of you, Miles. One would almost think you were trying to prevent me from distributing my casserole."

"I'm only trying to be practical," he said quickly.

Myrtle put her hands on her hips and studied the counter. "How about a compromise? I'll bring my casserole and a side of bread."

Miles looked slightly, if not totally, relieved.

Myrtle ended up persuading Miles to go to Orabelle's house with her, despite the somewhat early hour. He dragged his feet a bit as they walked up the front walk of the tidy, small home.

Myrtle decided to forego ringing the bell for a quieter knock, which made Miles breathe a sigh of relief.

A few minutes later, a groggy man in his early-forties peered through the door.

"Oh no," said Miles with a sigh.

"It was time for him to wake up anyway," said Myrtle in a no-nonsense tone. "It's practically midday."

Miles looked at his watch, saw it was nowhere near the noon hour, and stifled another sigh.

"Good morning," said Myrtle cheerily when Tripp opened the door. "Is your mother in?"

"Mom? Um, no, Miss Myrtle. No, she's already at the post office. Can I help you?" Tripp appeared to be waking up now, although his eyes were a little bleary.

"Goodness. I suppose we were just too late to catch her. Miles and I have brought a casserole for you and your mother to have for lunch or dinner."

Tripp looked at the casserole with some misgiving. Apparently, news of Myrtle's cooking escapades had reached his ears . . . likely from Orabelle.

"That's very nice of both of you," he said politely, carefully removing the offending casserole off Myrtle's hands.

Miles quickly inserted, "Actually, the food is from Myrtle. I'm just bringing my sympathy."

Tripp seemed to be hiding a smile. "Got it. Well, come on inside for a few minutes. Mom wouldn't like it if I just left you out on the doorstep."

"We're sorry we're here so early," said Miles stiffly as he followed Tripp inside.

"And very sorry about your uncle," added Myrtle, giving Tripp a sympathetic look.

Tripp nodded, looking solemn. "Thank you. Yes, it was a real shock for Mom and me. Really awful."

Myrtle and Miles sat down in the modest living room. Orabelle kept everything very tidy, Myrtle noted, and she wasn't at all surprised. If anyone was organized to the point of being uptight, it was Orabelle. But Tripp didn't seem to have the same proclivities for neatness. He immediately took off a sweatshirt and threw it on the back of a chair as he flopped on the sofa.

"So how are things going, Miss Myrtle?" asked Tripp.

Myrtle said, "Not too badly. Miles is trying to help me improve my chess game. He'll be sorely missing the games he played with Darren."

Tripp raised his eyebrows. "Oh, I didn't realize you two played together."

Miles asked, "Did you play with him?"

Tripp chuckled, dimples in both cheeks. "No way. I don't like losing and that's all I'd have done if I'd played with my uncle. No, I'm more of a poker guy and Darren didn't play poker."

"Does your mother?" asked Myrtle, looking startled.

He chuckled again. "No, ma'am. But we play gin rummy together."

"How special that must be. Such a comfort you must be to your mother." There was a slight sharpness in Myrtle's voice. Tripp was a former student and she didn't exactly remember him being this angelic. Quite the opposite, as a matter of fact. He was always charming, but could be duplicitous.

Miles mused, "Gin rummy. Haven't played that for a while."

"I treasure every minute," said Tripp.

Myrtle's eyes narrowed just a bit. "I'm sure your mother appreciates your being here, especially right now. She was very shaken up yesterday. I hope she was able to sleep last night."

Tripp said, "I don't know if she slept well or not. She wanted to go on to work today because otherwise she said she'd have too much time to think. I was glad I was home yesterday so I could be with her; you're right, she was pretty shaken up. We had a talk, then had a little cry and then we watched television and drank coffee. Mom was better later on."

"That's good to hear," said Myrtle. She paused, giving Tripp a sweet smile. "When will you be able to get your sunglasses back from the police?"

He gave her a startled look, eyes wide. "Excuse me?"

Miles stared at Myrtle.

"Oh, I noticed you'd left your sunglasses there at your uncle's house. Did you leave them there yesterday, or another day?" Myrtle kept smiling benignly at Tripp.

"Another day," muttered Tripp, not bothering to deny they were his glasses. He sighed. "Uncle Darren and I got along great. Things have been tight here, as you can imagine. Mom doesn't make a lot and I haven't exactly been contributing to household expenses with the job situation in Bradley being as it is. I popped over to talk to Uncle Darren and ask him for a loan."

Myrtle continued her smiling study of Tripp and he added shortly, "And it was a *loan* I was asking for. I fully expected to be able to pay him back as soon as I got a job."

"I suppose the reason you were interested in receiving funds from Darren is because of the windfall from his painting?" asked Myrtle.

Tripp snorted. "Of course. Can you believe it, Miss Myrtle? That painting wasn't even *pretty*. We're living in a time when an unsightly painting can bring in a ton of money."

"And was Darren amenable to lending you money?" asked Myrtle, still very sweetly.

He was leveling a suspicious look at Myrtle now, remembering she wasn't exactly this sweet in the classroom.

"No, actually, he wasn't. He had some hard words for me and all sorts of corny sayings he tossed my way. Told me idle hands were the devil's playthings." Tripp rolled his eyes. "That kind of thing. It was very annoying. And the thing that was the most annoying was that Uncle Darren hadn't put in an ounce of work to get the money."

Miles gave him a reproachful look and said reprovingly, "That's not entirely true, is it?"

Tripp leveled a look at Miles that was likely very much the same one he'd reserved for Darren. "Okay, you're right. He worked to clean out his attic. Then he found a painting . . . let me add a *hideous* painting, at that. Somehow, he thought the painting might be worth something and he made an appointment with an appraiser to find out. So he *sort of* worked to get that money. But he didn't work enough to make the huge amount of money he did. Maybe the work he invested in cleaning the attic might have been worth a couple of hundred dollars of pay."

Myrtle looked at him thoughtfully. "So the painting was hideous? I don't think anyone has admitted that."

Tripp rolled his eyes expressively. "It was awful. Nobody would dare say anything because the painting was worth so much and no one knows anything about art. But it's the kind of piece that punches you in the gut when you see it—in a bad way. This wasn't exactly a Monet. I wouldn't want it hanging in my house, that's for sure. We're living in a really weird time, is all I can say. A time where an ugly picture can bring in a million dollars."

Myrtle said, "Well, I don't know a lot about art, but it sounds as if someone found it very valuable. Do you think other people felt the way you did about your uncle? That he wasn't worthy of his windfall?"

Tripp shook his head. "I didn't say he wasn't worthy of it. I mean, he was a decent man. A good guy. I just said he didn't *work* for it, that's all. I didn't harbor any bad feelings toward him." He looked down then and Myrtle thought perhaps he had harbored just a *few* bad feelings when he'd been turned down for money. Tripp lifted his head again and continued. "I don't know how his friends and stuff felt about him suddenly being wealthy. How did you feel?" He directed his attention to Miles.

Miles looked startled to suddenly be the center of attention.

"Yes," said Myrtle sternly. "How did you feel, Miles?"

Miles cleared his throat. "I didn't really think about it one way or another. I believe I told Darren 'good for you' and that now he had options. He could do whatever he wanted to—travel, move to a bigger place, get a beach house. But he didn't seem to want to do anything with it. So we just kept on talking about books and playing chess. Pretty soon I forgot about it altogether."

Tripp pointed at him. "And that makes you a true friend. It didn't faze you at all. But I have the feeling you're not hurting for cash, either."

Miles looked uncomfortable. "I wouldn't say I *hurt* for it. I don't spend very much of it either, though."

Tripp shrugged. "Whatever. You don't need it or seem to want it. So you weren't jealous."

"Are you suggesting that other people were jealous, though?" asked Myrtle.

"I'm guessing they were. Why wouldn't they be? He not only got the money, he got all kinds of attention because the newspapers were writing about him," said Tripp.

"So you think someone killed him because they were jealous of his success?" Myrtle tilted her head at Tripp.

"No, I really *don't* think that. But who knows? I can tell you one person who wasn't real happy with my uncle, though." Tripp's eyes displayed cunning for a moment and Myrtle narrowed hers. This was more of the Tripp she remembered from school. And she had the feeling he was going to try to divert them from suspecting him or his mother.

"Who was that?" asked Myrtle.

"Carter Radnor," said Tripp.

Miles frowned. "The insurance agent?"

Myrtle said, "Not just an insurance agent. Pansy's good friend."

"Exactly," said Tripp. "And I kind of get the feeling he'd like to be more than Pansy's good friend."

Miles said slowly, "So he obviously wasn't too thrilled about Pansy's and Darren's relationship."

"You should have seen the looks he'd shoot my Uncle Darren. I bet now that he's dead, Carter is going to be lending Pansy his shoulder to cry on." Tripp smirked.

Myrtle said, "You're sure about that? I can't say I've seen Pansy and Carter together in a romantic way."

Tripp said, "I promise I know what I'm talking about. Carter spends as much time with Pansy as possible, trying to convince her he would be a better match than Darren. I hang out in town quite a bit and see him following her around like a puppy. Plus, I witnessed Carter having an argument with my uncle. I don't think it was over chess."

Miles said thoughtfully, "I don't believe Carter plays chess."

"Bingo," said Tripp, pointing at Miles.

"Definitely a lot of drama going on in Bradley." Myrtle stood and Miles and Tripp followed her lead.

"Always," said Tripp.

"Please tell your mother how sorry we are again," said Myrtle.

And they made their exit.

Miles and Myrtle got into Miles's car. Miles cast a sideways look at Myrtle. "You certainly asked a lot of leading questions back there."

Myrtle shrugged and put on her seatbelt. "He was a student of mine. I tend to fall back into old roles sometimes."

"What kind of student was he?" asked Miles as he pulled out of the driveway.

"Fair to middling," said Myrtle with a sniff. "He was charming, although he had a lazy streak a mile wide. Also, he could be rather duplicitous in the classroom. Always acting up and blaming someone else."

"That doesn't bode well for his possible involvement in Darren's death."

Myrtle said, "Who knows? People *can* change. It's just so rare that they do. Here's the problem Tripp is facing: he needs money. His uncle just made a good deal of money. He asked his uncle for money and was turned down. And his sunglasses were found at Darren's house. It sure doesn't look good for him."

"And he was eager to deflect attention from himself and toward Carter," added Miles.

"Carter still carries a flame for Pansy. Who'd have thought?" Myrtle looked over at Miles. "You didn't pick up on any of this after all the time you spent with Darren?"

Miles shook his head. "I told you, I was focusing more on improving my chess game. I was beginning to think Darren might find himself another chess partner if I didn't start getting any better. It's no fun to play with someone and win every time."

"Isn't it? I don't seem to find that's the case with Scrabble."

"*Anyway*," said Miles, "I don't really know much about all the drama surrounding Darren. It sounds as though he might have been getting sucked into some sort of love triangle." He made a face as if this was a very unsettling and unsavory thing for Darren to have done.

Chapter Eight

Miles pulled the car into his driveway and Myrtle raised her eyebrows. "I thought we were heading for my house."

"Let's come to mine and have brunch. It sounds like I might have more appropriate food in my house than you do."

"I have all those baked goods," protested Myrtle.

"For book club," reminded Miles.

"I've already had some breakfast this morning. With Elaine."

Miles said, "Maybe you can just have a little. That was a while back."

So they went into Miles's house and soon he'd made them eggs and bacon and some strong coffee since it would be a long day and they'd gotten an early start. Myrtle made a copy of the puzzle and comics page in the paper on Miles's printer and they worked the crossword puzzle at the same time.

Myrtle finished first and, pleased by her success, persuaded Miles to return to the chessboard where their game was still in progress. After she took Miles's rook, however, he glowered at her.

"What's wrong?" asked Myrtle in an innocent tone.

"You appear to be far better at this game than you'd indicated."

Myrtle shrugged. "If you say so. I haven't played in years. My dear departed husband and I used to play."

Miles's voice was accusatory. "You acted as if you didn't even know the name of the chess pieces!"

"Is it necessary to know the names of the pieces to win the game?"

Miles acknowledged this wasn't true and fumed for a few minutes until he realized he could take Myrtle's pawn.

She gave him a considering look. She'd set up the pawn as a trap and Miles had fallen right into it. "Perhaps we should give chess a break for a little while."

Miles glared at the board. "Maybe just for today. Apparently, my mind isn't quite with-it today."

Myrtle looked at her watch. "Heavens. Miles, we should head over to book club."

Miles didn't appear particularly enthusiastic about this suggestion. "It's pretty early."

"Yes, but I'm the person who suggested the library. I should make sure the community room is all set up with chairs out and tables for the food. And I'd like to put some props in the room, as well."

"Props?" Miles wrinkled his brow.

"Yes. Remember the underlying reason why I wanted to have the meeting at the library to begin with."

Miles said, "Because you wanted them to remember what book club is all about."

"Precisely. It's about *books*. It's not about alcohol. It's not about food. It's not about finding out what fabulous outfit Tippy is wearing and asking her where she got it. It's definitely not about catching up with local gossip."

Miles raised an eyebrow. "I thought one of the reasons we were going today was to catch up with local gossip . . . Pansy's, in particular."

"Well, okay, but that's because we're working to keep Bradley safe from a dangerous killer who is on the loose. We're doing it for *philanthropic* reasons. But besides that, we're trying to remind people that books are the basis of our club. Reading literature. Finishing the book."

Miles sighed. "Which I didn't. I didn't even know what the selection was."

"Of course you didn't. That's because the club has strayed from its original purpose to celebrate *literature*." Myrtle turned a critical eye to Miles's bookshelves. "I was going to do this at the library, but now I think it might be easier to simply raid your shelves."

Miles looked alarmed at this pronouncement. "Raid my shelves?"

Myrtle stood and swept over to the wall, studying the volumes of books. "Yes. Well, there's far too much Faulkner here, but we can take a representative tome. Perhaps *Absalom, Absalom.*" She plucked it from the shelf.

Myrtle frowned as she peered at his shelves. "You're rather fond of Thomas Hardy, too. Surprising."

Miles sounded defensive. "What's surprising about it?"

Myrtle ignored the question. "We'll skip *Jude, the Obscure* and bring *Tess of the d'Urbervilles*."

Her arms now full of rather heavy books, she thrust them at Miles.

"I'll find some tote bags," he said, a bit coldly.

Myrtle continued selectively pulling out books. She handed over *Anna Karenina*, *Wuthering Heights*, *Great Expectations*, *Animal Farm*, *Slaughterhouse Five*, and *The Picture of Dorian Gray*.

Miles shifted on his feet, looking sadly into the tote bags. "I want these books back in good condition, Myrtle."

She stared at him. "What on earth could possibly happen to them? We're at book club, not a bacchanalian festival."

Miles looked unhappily at her. "I remember a couple of times when book club descended into the realm of bacchanalia."

"Well, it's not going to happen today. There will be no alcohol at a library event, so that will nip all the bad players in the bud. We're going to discuss books. And murder." Myrtle saw her reflection in a mirror on Mile's wall. "Mercy! Miles, you didn't tell me my hair was standing up on end like Einstein's."

Miles tilted his head to one side. "I don't think I really noticed it."

"Okay, well, it clearly needs attention. I need to go home for a few minutes anyway to get the food I'm bringing. Since we're carrying so much stuff, we should drive to the library instead of walking there."

"I'll pick you up in ten minutes," said Miles, looking gloomily down at the bags of his books.

Fifteen minutes later, they were at the library. The front desk unlocked the community room for Myrtle and she strode in. "Let's see. I think we should change the configuration of the tables a little so everyone isn't at the front of the room. Let's have the food table to the left and the drinks table to the right."

Miles looked alarmed. "I thought you said there weren't going to *be* any drinks."

"Non-alcoholic beverages. Tippy is responsible for bringing them this month, I believe. The chairs are all good. Now, let's scatter the books around. They're the most important part of the meeting, after all. I happened to bring some plate stands from home to put the books on." Myrtle dug in her huge purse and pulled out the wooden plate stands.

Myrtle and Miles set the books up on plate stands on the two tables. Then Myrtle took Elaine's baking out and put it on one of the tables.

Tippy, president of the book club, bustled in with bags of her own. As usual, she was wearing an elegant outfit . . . this time in black and white. Her face was perfectly made-up and she was very organized. The only annoying thing about Tippy in regard to the book club was that she picked ridiculous books when it was her turn to select one.

She smiled at them both. "You're here early. Thanks for setting this up, Myrtle. The library is a great idea."

Myrtle said, "Oh, I thought it was time to go back to our roots, you know. *Books.*" She threw a scornful look at Tippy's selection for the month.

Tippy seemed oblivious to Myrtle's antipathy for the novel. She lowered her brows and studied the room's set-up. "Okay, so it looks like we're putting beverages on this table, here."

Miles watched unhappily as 2-liter bottles of Coca-Cola, cups, and an ice bucket were placed perilously close to his precious tomes.

Myrtle asked in a carefully careless way, "Is Pansy making it today? I know yesterday was a bad day for her."

Tippy said, "A really miserable day. I felt so terrible for her. She said that just hanging around her house was making her crazy, though—she kept thinking about Darren. I persuaded her to come to book club and be distracted for a little while."

Myrtle nodded. She had no doubt that Tippy was able to accomplish this. Tippy, for one, was used to getting her way.

A few other book club members came in, one of them Georgia Simpson. She was a tattooed former student of Myrtle's with big hair. She collected ceramic and glass angels, and was an object of fascination for Miles, who had met someone quite like her when he served in Vietnam.

Georgia came straight over to Myrtle. "Got something for ya."

"Do you?" asked Myrtle with interest. She was accustomed to Georgia's "finds" from various flea markets and garage sales. However, it could be *anything*. Georgia's finds were usually only treasures in her own mind. Once she'd found a coffin and transformed it into a coffee table. Myrtle certainly hoped it wasn't another case of creative repurposing that Georgia had in mind.

"Sure do. It's in the back of my truck. Want to come see it?"

Myrtle decidedly did *not* want to see it, but she didn't have a wonderful excuse not to. The room was definitely set up and book club hadn't started yet. Pansy was nowhere to be seen. So she stifled a sigh and tried to garner some enthusiasm as she followed Georgia outside. Miles gave her a curious look, but he was caught up in conversation with a gaggle of book club women (and keeping an eye on his books).

"Here we go!" said Georgia, looking proudly at a tremendous gnome taking up most of the bed of her pickup truck.

Myrtle gaped at it. "It's huge!"

Someone, apparently, didn't ultimately grasp the *concept* of a gnome. The fact that it was *small*. Sort of like Santa. Santa was supposed to be an *elf*. Somehow, Santa had morphed into a really large full-sized man over the years.

The gnome grinned sassily at her. It had his hands on his hips, wore overalls, and had a pipe in his mouth. Its color had faded through the years and it had a rather greenish tint. It looked more like the Jolly Green Giant than a gnome.

"Ain't it a beaut?" asked Georgia. "Saw it and thought of you immediately. The former owners couldn't keep it anymore, so they gave it to me for free when they heard about your collection. They just wanted it to have a good home."

As if it were a gerbil or an unexpected puppy or kitten in the house. But still . . .

"I love it," said Myrtle firmly.

A grin spread across Georgia's features and she gave a knowing nod. "Figured you would."

"I actually have a . . . situation . . . going on right now that this gnome would be perfect for."

"Red givin' you trouble?" asked Georgia sharply. Her tone didn't bode well for Red if she were to see him.

"In a manner of speaking," said Myrtle. "You know how he likes to be pushy. Anyway, I think this gnome, positioned perfectly in the yard, will make my point." The gnome, grinning around the pipe, seemed to agree with her.

Georgia nodded again. "You're going to need some help with this guy, though. I had to really wrestle him to get him in the truck."

"My Dusty is allegedly setting out my gnomes right now and should be able to take care of this once we get him to my house."

Georgia looked at her watch. "We don't want to miss him, then. Maybe I should just scoot over there real quick, have Dusty help dump him out of the truck, and run back over here."

"Perhaps that would be best. And thank you, Georgia." Myrtle hurried back into book club as Georgia fired up her truck and sped off.

Pansy had shown up during Myrtle's interlude with Georgia and was currently the center of a very sympathetic crowd of women.

Miles came over. "What did Georgia want?" he asked curiously.

"Oh, she had a gnome for me. She's heading back to my house to hand it over to Dusty." She glanced at the gaggle of ladies around Pansy. "Help me clear those women out so I can speak with Pansy before book club starts."

Miles frowned. "Clear them out? What on earth do you want me to do?"

Myrtle sighed. "Don't act as if you don't know your magical powers with my book club. Stand near them and start talking to one of them. The rest will automatically flock over."

Miles nervously eyed the group of older women. "Which one should I start with? And what should I talk about?"

"For heaven's sake, Miles, just pick one! It doesn't even matter what you say. She'll be charmed, delighted and simpering, the same as always."

Miles, looking more like a man facing a bloody battle and certain death than one approaching a woman of advanced years, bravely strode toward the group before he could think it over more. On the way, he grabbed a cup of punch (Tippy had apparently efficiently mixed up a batch while Myrtle had been outside) and squared his shoulders as he approached them. He thrust the cup at a punch-less book club attendee in the group who gave him a delighted smile and turned toward him. Like lemmings, the rest of the huddle shifted their attention to Miles.

Myrtle walked over and removed Pansy from the group with surgical precision. She gave her a sweet smile, the type she reserved for just such occasions.

"Pansy, dear. How are you holding up? I wanted to let you know how very, very sorry I was to hear about poor Darren."

Pansy nodded. Her eyes were still rather bloodshot, but she seemed to be otherwise in good shape, to Myrtle's relief. Myrtle was never a fan of crying and was very glad she wasn't going to have to proffer Pansy a tissue. "I'm doing all right, Myrtle. I hear you and Miles found Darren there. That must have been awful."

"Well, he was in the attic as you know, dear. I'm afraid I didn't trust myself on those attic stairs with my cane and whatnot. But Miles, yes, he was quite distraught. He's much better today, though."

"Yes, I can see that," said Pansy a bit dryly as she observed the women flirting with Miles and Miles's blushing face.

"I was going to make you a casserole," said Myrtle.

Pansy looked alarmed. "That's not necessary, Myrtle."

Chapter Nine

Myrtle smiled reassuringly at her. "You don't have to look so worried, Pansy. It's no imposition at all. I've already made one for Orabelle and Tripp."

"Really, Myrtle, it's fine. I've gotten so much food already that I may never eat it all."

Myrtle said, "Have you? As I was *going* to say, I've found myself in a situation where funds are rather tight until the end of the week and the casserole would have to wait a bit. But if you're sure you're covered?"

"Absolutely sure," said Pansy firmly.

Myrtle nodded and then said, "I'm thrilled you managed to make it to book club. It must be good to have something as a distraction right now."

"You're right. It's been a terrible last 24-hours. Tippy told me not to bring anything to book club, but I couldn't help myself. I wanted to do something to stay busy, so I made some cookies to bring." She reached over to the nearby table and plucked a cookie off the plate. "Here, try one."

Myrtle obediently took a bite and then struggled not to make a face. Something had gone terribly wrong with that cookie. Had she left out sugar? Had she substituted some other white powdery kitchen ingredient by accident? The cookie was vile.

Pansy didn't seem to notice that Myrtle wasn't taking any further bites from the offending cookie. She continued, "I just feel so terrible that there I was, getting ready for my day, and Darren was fighting for his life." She shuddered and struggled to regain control of her emotions.

Myrtle decided to move on to a slightly different topic in the hopes of keeping Pansy's tears at bay. "Miles mentioned that Carter has been a good friend to you through all this," she fibbed, throwing Miles under the proverbial bus. Miles narrowed his eyes at her from across the room as if he somehow knew what she was saying.

Pansy blinked at her in surprise. "Carter? Well, he hasn't been in touch with me for a couple of days. Poor Carter. He's always been such a kind friend. And he's been so lonely since his wife passed away."

Myrtle said, "So you two have always just been friends, then."

Pansy said sadly, "I just never thought of Carter *that* way. Not in a romantic way."

"He wanted you to, though?"

Pansy nodded and said in a conspiratorial whisper, "Poor Carter was terribly upset with Darren. He thought he'd be a much better boyfriend than Darren was." She hesitated and colored a little. "He had an awful argument with Darren just recently. He was quite violent and unlike himself. You know he's usually so sweet."

Myrtle, in fact, did *not* know this. Carter Radnor always seemed rather intense to her. He'd always struck her as a workaholic. She was surprised to discover that he had another side to him.

"What did they argue over?" asked Myrtle.

Pansy batted her lashes modestly. "Over me. Can you believe it, Myrtle? But it wasn't the romantic thing it's always portrayed as in books. Not a bit like two knights fighting over a fair maiden. It was just awful. Those were two people I cared about and they were both shouting at each other."

"Goodness, that must have been very upsetting." Although Myrtle couldn't quite manage to sound convincing on that point. "And it must have been upsetting, as well, that Carter wasn't really listening to you when you told him you preferred to stay with Darren. Which you *did*, I presume."

Pansy quickly said, "Oh, yes. Many times. And anyone could see that Darren and I had a special relationship. I always thought he and I would end up at the altar together. We got along so well and had so much in common."

"Chess?" asked Myrtle dubiously.

Pansy gave a light laugh. "Maybe not chess."

Myrtle smiled at her. "Well, it certainly sounds like a *lovely* relationship. That's so unusual, isn't it? Too often couples have spats and things, don't they?" Like Orabelle mentioned that Pansy and Darren had had.

Pansy kept her unwavering and brave smile. "Yes. What a pity about that. People need to remember the love that was the basis for their partnership to begin with."

Myrtle said, "So you were very supportive of him when he discovered the painting in his attic, then, I'm guessing. Happy for him. It was quite an amazing find, I understand."

"Oh, yes. Yes, I was very happy for him. I mean, the painting wasn't pretty at all and I didn't think it could possibly be worth anything when Darren first showed it to me. But I was happy to admit I was wrong after he got it appraised. And then the attention from the magazine was so *good* for him and he was so proud! I was even quoted in one of the periodicals," she said, flushing a little with pleasure at the memory.

"Isn't that so very wonderful?" said Myrtle.

Pansy seemed to realize there might be the very slightest edge to Myrtle's question. She flushed again, this time in annoyance. "You, of course, are in the paper all the time, aren't you? I think you wrote the article on Darren this morning." She grudgingly added, "It was a good piece."

"Thanks," said Myrtle. She said, "I'm hoping that, as the town's investigative reporter, I can help track down who did this to Darren.

Pansy blinked at her, then quickly glanced over Myrtle's form . . . from the top of her gray head to the cane she held sturdily in one hand, to her sensible orthopedic shoes. "That's, well, that's remarkable."

"Yes. And considering this mission of mine . . . do you have any ideas as to who might have harbored such feelings of ill-will toward Darren?"

Pansy looked down as she thought. Myrtle carefully held the horrid cookie behind her back as she did. "Everyone liked Darren. They really did."

Myrtle said carefully, "Dear, *no one* is liked by everyone." She paused. "Do you know anything, by the way, about a potential connection between Darren and someone named Liam?"

"Liam Hudson? Yes. He was Darren's lawyer. As a matter of fact, he mentioned something about him a couple of days ago. I got the impression he was somewhat at odds with him."

Myrtle frowned. "Why would Darren be at odds with his lawyer?"

"I don't really know. I just know Darren kept saying Liam wasn't who he appeared," said Pansy. "He mentioned that maybe he could find proof."

"How very ambiguous of Darren! What on earth did he mean by that?"

Pansy shrugged a thin shoulder.

"You didn't ask?" Myrtle found some people's absence of curiosity quite amazing.

"No. I think I was busy at the time. Yes, I was shucking corn."

Myrtle thought shucking corn was a very poor substitute to finding out more information on a really mysterious statement by one's boyfriend. "And that was *all* he said on the matter?"

Pansy's brow furrowed even further as if she were reaching into the very soles of her feet to try to think of what else Darren might have said. She slowly added, "No, he said one thing more. I didn't really understand where he was going with it. He said it was the same time as the big snowstorm."

"Big snowstorm? Here in Bradley?" A big snowstorm in the North Carolina town might be interpreted as one that actually dusted the ground instead of merely elevated surfaces. Even a small amount of white stuff was usually enough to bring the entire town to a screeching halt. And wipe grocery store shelves free of bread and milk.

"Or hurricane?" added Pansy, unhelpfully.

Myrtle sighed. Pansy was clearly not the fount of information she could be.

"No, wait. It was *definitely* a hurricane. That's because Darren and I started talking about where we were at the time it hit."

Since Bradley wasn't a coastal town, but hours away from the beach, this did help limit possibilities. The number of hurricanes that had any sort of impact on the town were few and far between. "Could it have been Hurricane Hugo?" asked Myrtle.

"Hmm. No. At least, I don't think so. Darren said it was when he was living in Boston at the time. It was a hurricane that impacted his area there."

Tippy joined them then. "May I borrow Pansy now, Myrtle?"

Myrtle nodded and Tippy whisked her away; perhaps because Pansy's furrowed brow and worried expression as she tried to pull up memories made Tippy think Myrtle was somehow making Pansy unhappy. And, judging from Tippy's censorious look, unhappiness at book club was against the rules.

Miles walked up to Myrtle and she thrust the half-eaten cookie into his hand surreptitiously. "Get rid of this for me, would you?"

Miles did, and then covered his hands with the bottle of sanitizer he conveniently had in the pocket of his khakis. "What was that?" he asked.

"A ghastly culinary misstep by Pansy," said Myrtle. She rubbed her hand clean on her slacks.

Miles said, "Well, I suppose she might be distracted. Under the circumstances."

"I'm not entirely sure she doesn't bake like that all the time," said Myrtle.

Miles narrowed his eyes. "Sometimes people don't realize how bad their cooking is."

"They should be pitied for their lack of self-perception," said Myrtle with a sniff.

Miles looked to be on the point of elaborating on this subject, when Myrtle's cell phone started ringing. She startled. "Who on earth could be calling me?" she muttered, fumbling to retrieve the phone from her voluminous purse.

She glanced at it and then answered. "Red! I'm at book club. It's really not a very good time."

"I could say the same," grated Red. "I'm in the middle of a murder investigation and yet I'm getting citizen complaints about a large gnome blocking the sidewalk in front of my mother's house."

"A large gnome? How silly. And the perfect example of an oxymoron."

"And yet it seems to be true. I've received several calls."

Myrtle glanced across the room at Georgia and caught her eye. Georgia gave her a thumbs-up and a grin. Myrtle supposed she was to interpret those gestures to mean Georgia had somehow offloaded the gnome. Apparently onto a public walkway.

"Mama, there's a town ordinance against blocking a sidewalk."

"I've done no such thing! I've been at book club for the last forty-five minutes; setting up the room and speaking with fellow literature-lovers. Ask anyone."

Red growled, "I'm tied up right now, but then I'm going to have to address this giant gnome. I'm thinking about giving you a ticket, too."

"Whatever. I have to go." Myrtle hung up just as Tippy was clapping her hands to get the attention of the group.

"Ladies and gentleman," Tippy said winking and smiling at Miles. "I want to welcome everyone to our book club. Let's extend a special welcome to Pansy Denham, who's just joining us."

Everyone beamed at Pansy and gave her a round of applause. She teared up a bit at this and Tippy expertly diverted attention away from her again.

"And thanks, also, to Myrtle, who had the brainstorm for us to hold this month's meeting at the library. Perhaps Myrtle would like to say a few words about this?"

Myrtle decided she would. She stood up and walked to the front of the room. She summoned her classroom voice from years ago. It was a necessary voice to utilize since there were still two members whispering to each other in the back, another seemingly mesmerized by the snack table, and yet another busily spilling punch on the table and one of Miles's precious books. Miles gaped in horror from across the room.

Myrtle cleared her throat and said, "The reason I wanted us to meet at the library this month was to remind our group what book club is all about."

"Books!" beamed one of the members, as if she were the teacher's pet and wanted a gold star.

Myrtle gave her a reproving look at interrupting. "That's true. And while we *do* talk about books, I feel we've somehow lost our way. We've become too interested in socializing." She gave a significant pause here and stared at the two women who were still whispering together. They blushed and stopped. "We must find our way back to real literature. For inspiration, I've picked out some wonderful books from Miles's own personal library."

The woman who'd just sloshed punch on one of Miles's books also blushed and scrubbed furiously at the red stain on the front cover of *Ivanhoe*.

Blanche raised her hand and Myrtle nodded at her. "Are there any classic novels that are actually easy reading? Because the last thing I want to do with my free time is to work hard at relaxing."

There was murmured assent from the group and Myrtle raised a hand, stopping the murmurings in their tracks.

"Certainly there are," said Myrtle smoothly, walking over to the table with *Tess of the d'Urbervilles*. But she was interrupted by, of all people, Erma.

"I know the *best* book for us to read," she chirped up.

Everyone turned to look at her.

"I do, I really do! I got to the library early and I went over to see what might be good for us to read."

"Is it your month to pick?" asked Myrtle through gritted teeth. She sincerely hoped it wasn't.

"I've *never* picked," said Erma beaming. "I've always let other people have my turn."

Tippy cleared her throat. "Well, then, I think we should let Erma determine what book we read for next month."

Erma nodded. She glanced around at everyone's eyes on her and preened.

"Let's have it, Erma," said Myrtle grimly, steeling herself for the title.

"*Frankenstein*," said Erma.

Myrtle said, "All right. By Mary Shelley. That's actually not a bad choice for the group. An excellent gothic tale that we're all somewhat familiar with. But it has a good deal of depth, too."

Erma nodded enthusiastically. "Yes! But it gets even better. I found they have a graphic novel version here at the library. They have quite a few copies, so it must be popular. Then I looked online and there were plenty of used copies, too, for hardly any money. Won't that be so much fun?"

The book club seemed to think that was a *lot* of fun. They liked the idea of being able to see the monster and the doctor. They asked what other books the library had as graphic novels and Erma was able to go into a great deal of detail as to the library's fairly extensive collection.

Myrtle walked back to her seat and Miles looked at her sympathetically. "This wasn't exactly how you wanted things to go."

"No."

Miles said, "But, you know, it may end up that this will lead to the group tackling some good books after they've read a condensed format."

"Miles, I have no hope at all that's what's going to end up happening. Let's move on."

Tippy was clapping her hands again and started the discussion of that month's pick: a maudlin little tale of a middle-aged woman battling the inevitable tide of aging. Myrtle rolled her eyes. She'd mastered aging and it was irritating to her to hear about anyone who was struggling with the process.

As it happened, it seemed no one had really read the book. This was excellent news because the actual discussion portion of the meeting was cut short. Then everyone started milling around and visiting again.

Miles said, "Can we get out of here? You've already spoken with Pansy." He looked with misgivings as another book club member picked up one of his books while juggling a chocolate doughnut someone had brought in. He winced as she flipped through the pages.

"Yes, let's get out while the getting is good," muttered Myrtle.

"Too late," said Miles glumly as a woman waved at them and started walking over with great determination.

Chapter Ten

"Sherry," said Myrtle with a sigh. "She's fond of chatting, too. We may never make it out of here alive."

"Hi, you two," said Sherry cheerfully. "Say, I haven't seen either of you at the gym lately. What gives?"

Sherry worked at the gym and also worked *out* at the gym.

Miles quickly said, "My knee has been giving me trouble lately."

Myrtle raised her eyebrows innocently. "Goodness, *has* it, Miles? You've been so very stoic about it that I didn't even realize."

He glared at her. "Why haven't *you* made it to the gym, Myrtle?"

"Me? Why I've been just so terribly busy. You know how I write investigative reports for the newspaper." Myrtle glanced at Pansy across the room and lowered her voice. "Yesterday's news has kept me hopping."

Sherry nodded solemnly. "Got it. Isn't it awful? You know I live right next door to Orabelle. She seemed just devastated yesterday when I spoke with her. She and Darren have always been so close."

Myrtle said, "And I suppose you're also a neighbor of Tripp's, since he's living with his mother now."

Sherry made a face. "I suppose I am. Although I think he should think about himself a little less and spend more time thinking about his mother. I see Orabelle lugging the trash out all by herself every day. I bet most of the trash is Tripp's, too, because I always see him bringing in fast food bags." She sighed.

Miles said slowly, "He seemed rather nice when I met him."

"Don't get me wrong; he's charming. But I think he might be trouble, too," said Sherry.

Myrtle nodded. "That's hard on Orabelle, especially right now. Maybe he'll start looking after his mama better since she's going through such a challenging time." She paused. "I hear Tripp was home yesterday when Darren was found."

Sherry put her hands on her hips. "He certainly was *not*. His car hadn't been over there for a whole day at that point. I remember because I thought 'Oh, maybe he's *finally* moved back out. It was only supposed to be a temporary thing, but there he was camping out at his mom's."

Sherry seemed prepared to lecture at length on Tripp's general ineptitude at being a good son, so Myrtle quickly interrupted. "You're saying he *wasn't* at home."

"He was *not*. And I told Red that same thing. It happened to be my day off from the gym yesterday, so I was there. But you know how it is—when you're used to waking up early, you keep on waking up early. I'm usually at the gym at 6 a.m. and so I'm up at 5 or earlier. I went out to get my paper and I saw Tripp *still* wasn't there."

Someone called out to her and she gave them both a smile. "Good talking to y'all! Take care, now. And come back to the gym!"

Miles waved at her and said in an urgent undertone, "*Now* we should go."

But going didn't seem to be in the cards yet. Georgia Simpson sauntered up to them. "Y'all trying to escape?" she boomed with a hearty laugh. She saw their stricken faces and chuckled, "Hey, don't worry. I won't hold you up. Just wanted to give you an update on the gnome, Myrtle. Delivery went as well as could be expected since your guy wasn't there."

Myrtle looked vexed. "What? Dusty wasn't there? He *said* he'd be there."

"Nope. But there were signs he'd already been by your place. *Lots* of signs. There were gnomes crammed into just about every available spot on your lawn. I didn't have time to rearrange them so I could put that big guy in there. Plus, I'm not going to lie, that dude was pretty heavy. So I just heaved him out of my truck and put him right there on the sidewalk. Anyway, I'll let you and Miles head on out. See ya later." She strode off, tattooed arms swinging as she went.

"I'm starting to wonder if I dare to collect my books or whether we'll be accosted again," fretted Miles.

"Go get the car. I've got a tote bag I can stick everything in and dangle it from my arm."

Miles frowned. "That might make me appear un-chivalrous."

"Yes, but you're also the major draw between the two of us. We'll never get out of here if you don't leave," said Myrtle.

Five minutes later, she joined him in the car with a bag of books. Elaine's food was all gone, so she'd just thrown away the paper plates it rested on.

"Where to?" asked Miles.

"Let's drive back to my house. I can fill you in and then we can watch *Tomorrow's Promise*."

Miles headed in that direction. When he pulled up to Myrtle's house, he said, "What's *that*?"

Myrtle smirked. "It appears to be a man grappling with an oversized gnome."

"Is that *Red*?"

"Yes. I didn't have a chance to tell you that Georgia gave me a gnome she'd come across. She left it on the sidewalk instead of trying to find a better spot for it. Apparently, it's heavy."

Miles continued staring at Red, now waltzing with the gnome as he tried to maneuver it off the public sidewalk. "Apparently so."

Red finally wrestled it off the sidewalk and walked it backward into Myrtle's grass. He stepped back and wiped sweat from his brow, then spotted Myrtle and Miles. He glowered at Myrtle as she nonchalantly stepped from the car and pulled out her house keys.

"Mama! What's the meaning of this? You know you can't put your things on the public right-of-way!"

Myrtle pursed her lips and gave Red a reproving look. "As if I would do any such thing, Red Clover. You think *I* could have put that gnome there? You could barely move it, yourself."

Red rubbed the side of his head as if an incipient headache was making itself known there. "I think one of your minions did it for you. By the look of your front yard, I'm guessing Dusty."

"Actually, it was Georgia Simpson. But she had no plans at all for blocking the sidewalk."

Red growled, "Well, for someone who had no plans, she sure did a good job."

Myrtle said, "She was simply giving me the gnome as a gift and had a hard time managing it or finding a free spot in the grass."

Red put his hands on his hips and surveyed the gnome. "This is the King Kong of gnomes. It's got to go, Mama. I mean, the other gnomes are tacky, but this one takes the cake. It's a public nuisance by its very existence. Get rid of it."

"I'll do no such thing. Georgia would be devastated."

Miles smiled at the unlikely scenario of brash Georgia having her feelings hurt.

Red said, "Georgia would be *devastated*? We're talking about the same Georgia, aren't we?"

"She would. It would be unkind of me to get rid of her gift. Georgia is a dear friend."

Red narrowed his eyes. "Since when?"

"Since always. Miles and I have always held her in high regard."

Miles raised his eyebrows at this, but quickly nodded in agreement.

Red now rubbed his eyes with his two hands as if the headache had migrated there. "I give up. Do whatever you like with the thing . . . with the exception of allowing him on the sidewalk. But if I start getting complaints from the citizens of Bradley, I'll let you know."

He started stomping back to his police cruiser in his driveway across the street. Myrtle sang after him, "See you at supper tonight!"

Red stopped in his tracks. "Supper?"

"Yes. Remember the state of my pocketbook? The sad lack of funds? I'll be eating at your house. Elaine said she'd be delighted to have me there."

Red's face as he turned back around indicated that he didn't share his wife's feelings whatsoever.

Myrtle pranced inside with Miles following.

Miles said, "I'm glad I'm not the one having supper with Red tonight."

"Oh, he'll calm down. He always does. Now, do we want anything to eat? I still have some odds and ends here." She walked into the kitchen and looked doubtfully inside the pantry. "Sardines? Olives?"

Miles quickly shook his head. "Not for me. I ate at book club."

Myrtle made a face. "All I had there was Pansy's yucky cookie. I think I'll snack on some granola bars."

They settled down in the living room and Myrtle picked up the remote, but then laid it in her lap. "Before we watch the show, I'd like to run over what we know about the case so far."

"We know things?" Miles sounded rather dubious on this point.

"Of course we do! You just haven't been paying attention, Miles. Let me recount it for you."

"Please do," said Miles, settling down on Myrtle's sofa.

Myrtle looked pleased at having an audience. It reminded her of her days in the classroom. "First off, we know Tripp Whitley was at Darren's house. We know he asked his uncle for money and that Darren sent him off with a flea in his ear."

Miles frowned. "Do we really know all that? It seems rather a leap. I think we really only *know* Tripp asked for money and Darren refused to give it to him."

"Whatever," said Myrtle, waving away the pesky details with her hand. "We know Tripp thinks Carter Radnor was upset with Darren because Carter wants to date Pansy. Speaking to Carter should be one of our next orders of business."

Miles considered this and nodded. "Agreed."

Myrtle continued, "We know Orabelle Whitley is very protective of her son and he does no wrong in her eyes."

Miles wrinkled his brow. "Again, that's something of a stretch. She seemed to be a concerned mother to me, yes. But it didn't seem like she thought Tripp did no wrong."

"She wanted to swipe those sunglasses before the police spotted them. Perkins was simply too fast for her. And Sherry didn't seem to think Tripp was all that great of a son."

Miles shrugged. "Just because Tripp doesn't take the trash out. Sherry has a way of over-simplifying things."

"A grown man like Tripp—a man in his 40s—should certainly not allow his elderly mother to haul trash around while he's living in her house. Red Clover gets on my last nerve, but every Tuesday like clockwork he rolls my dumpster to the side of the road and back. And he doesn't even live in the same building."

Miles said, "Granted. However, I think it's quite a big step from him being a slouch of a son to him murdering his uncle."

Myrtle narrowed her eyes at him. "You're being quite obstreperous, Miles."

"I'm simply playing devil's advocate."

"Well *stop*."

Miles sighed. "Okay. So let's see. That takes care of Tripp and I guess Orabelle. Although I didn't quite understand what Orabelle's motive was. She killed Darren to protect Tripp somehow?"

"No, no. She killed Darren for money. She was angry with him for denying her son money and things got out of hand."

"Things got so out of hand that she clocked him with a flashlight?" Miles sounded doubtful on this point.

"You're doing it again!"

"Sorry, sorry. I think I just want to make sure to respect Darren's memory by not going after his family if they're innocent; that's all." Miles looked penitent this time.

"All right," growled Myrtle. "We might figure out a better motive for Orabelle later on. So let's move on to non-family-members."

"Excellent."

Myrtle said, "We have Pansy, Darren's girlfriend. We have Carter, part of Darren's love triangle."

Miles chuckled.

Myrtle said, "Yes, Miles? Is there something you wanted to interject?"

"It just amuses me to think of crusty old Darren in the middle of a love triangle." Miles's eyes danced at the thought.

She gave him a reproving look. "Then we have Pansy, herself."

"I might have missed why Pansy is a suspect."

"Because she was Darren's girlfriend. It's so frequently the spouse or significant other. Besides, Darren's newfound wealth makes all sorts of financial motives possible."

Miles looked surprised. "You think Darren might have left money to Pansy in his will?"

"Who knows? Maybe Pansy thought he would. And then we have Liam."

Miles pushed his glasses up. "Liam? Is he the lawyer Red mentioned?"

"Bingo."

"And why is he a suspect? I must have missed something again," said Miles. "I only know Darren mentioned something about him. He didn't say Liam was on the premises or anything."

"You weren't privy to the conversation Pansy and I had at book club. When I wasn't choking down the cookie, Pansy told me that there was something Darren had realized about Liam. It all seemed to involve a hurricane."

Miles's eyebrows shot up. "A *hurricane*?"

"Or perhaps a snowstorm. At any rate, Liam might have been upset with Darren because he knew something from years before. A secret. Pansy thought that Darren said something about finding proof that Liam wasn't who he said he was. So Liam is also on our list of people to track down and speak with." After making this point, Myrtle paused. She looked down at the granola bars in her lap.

"Change of plans," she said briskly, standing back up and putting the granola bars carefully back in her kitchen pantry for later.

"What are we doing?" asked Miles.

"I think we should speak to Liam now." Myrtle grabbed her large pocketbook and cane and started walking toward the door.

"Speaking with a lawyer might be an expensive proposition. They tend to charge by the hour." Miles stayed put on the sofa. He cast the television a longing look.

"Don't worry. *Tomorrow's Promise* will still be here when we get back. And we don't have to go to Liam's office. I bet you anything he'll be at Bo's Diner. His law office is directly next door and he's at the diner all the time. He'll be happy to talk to us."

Miles seemed doubtful on this point, but stood up. "Did you teach him, too?"

"Not Liam. He's from Somewhere Else. I'm just not sure where that somewhere is. Although I'm wondering if it might be Boston since Darren lived there with his wife for a while."

They walked back to Miles's car and climbed in. Miles glanced over at her as he started off down the street. "I thought you were trying not to spend money this week."

"Well, I don't have enough for another grocery shopping trip, but I *should* have enough for a five-dollar meal at the diner. Besides, I'm starving. It's not as if I don't have a cent to my name. I probably could come up with five dollars by rummaging around in my sofa cushions." Myrtle considered this. "Actually, that's not a bad idea. I'll have to try that when I come back."

Bo's Diner was very crowded this time.

"Looks like we're going to have to wait a while," said Miles gloomily.

Myrtle was scanning the restaurant and honed in on Liam. "There he is. All by himself." She started walking in that direction.

Miles muttered, "Myrtle, it doesn't look like he wants company. You're not proposing we join him?"

But Myrtle was already at the booth. She beamed at Liam, giving him her very best shaky old-lady smile. "Hi there, Liam. Do you mind if Miles and I sit at your table? It's just that the wait is very long and I'm very old and my blood sugar levels get all messed up when I don't eat regularly. Goodness, I might just pass out on the floor." She gave a convincing wobble.

Liam, a handsome man in his 40s, rose quickly to his feet. "Of course," he said politely, although Myrtle detected a hint of annoyance in his eyes.

She and Miles settled into the booth across from him.

Chapter Eleven

The waitress came right up to join them. Myrtle said, "A pimento cheese dog and an iced tea, please."

Miles ordered the chicken salad plate.

Myrtle smiled at Liam. "You are so kind to let us sit here. I'm sure you have other, very important business matters to attend to. Notes to look through. Phone calls to make." Myrtle made a vague gesture with her hands meant to encompass the daily tasks of the entire law profession.

Liam said in a light tone, "Oh, nothing that can't be put off for a little while. Especially for the town matriarch."

Myrtle wasn't altogether sure she liked that particular designation, but she gave a pleased cluck just the same. Miles gave a snorting chuckle and Myrtle gave him a kick under the table.

Myrtle twinkled her eyes at Liam and said, "You know, I've always been so interested in language and dialect. I think of myself as something of a local expert. At any rate, I can usually tell when someone grew up very close to Bradley or when someone spent most of their life in a different place, like Miles. But I just can't seem to place your accent. Where are you originally from?"

Liam seemed to wish they were back talking about town matriarchs instead of this alarming offshoot of the conversation.

"Oh, I'm a New York guy. Born and bred there," he said with a quick smile.

"*Are* you? I'm certainly less-confident about my dialect-gauging talents for other parts of the country, but I could have sworn you have a Bostonian accent," said Myrtle sweetly. "Don't you agree, Miles?"

Miles bobbed his head. "I sure do."

Liam's eyes grew a bit colder. He said stiffly, "My father was from Boston. Perhaps that's why I carry traces of the accent."

"You've never been there?" asked Miles.

"No." Liam took out his wallet pointedly and gathered up his phone as if preparing to leave.

Miles said, "I had a friend who spent time in Boston. Did you know Darren Powell at all?"

Liam rested his phone back down on the table. "I'm not from Boston."

Myrtle said, "But you knew Darren."

"Of course I did," he said, his genial demeanor now becoming irritated. "We live in a tiny town. I know nearly everyone."

"Was Darren a client of yours?" asked Myrtle.

"Attorney-client privilege," said Liam with a sniff.

Miles said thoughtfully, "Which you couldn't claim unless Darren was a client and you were his lawyer."

Liam leaned over the table and hissed at them, "What's this about, then?" His tone was icy and he glanced around the room to see if anyone was listening in.

Myrtle used her very own icy voice. "I'm simply asking an innocent question. However, now it's apparent that there is *something* there. Did you and Darren not get along? Was there a problem between the two of you? Would you care to comment?"

"On what authority are you asking questions?" he asked, a pompous expression on his face. "You're just a nosy old woman."

"And the crime desk reporter for the *Bradley Bugle*," growled Myrtle. She decided she might as well go whole-hog. "I've heard from several sources that you had an altercation with Darren Powell. I'd very much like to hear more about it. How did you know him? Can you offer a perspective on Darren for my upcoming story?"

Liam gave an uncomfortable laugh. "I only had business dealings with Darren related to the sale of the painting he'd found in his attic. I knew nothing about him."

"Even in a small town where everyone knows everyone else?" asked Miles, frowning.

Myrtle said, "We're trying to help figure out what happened to Darren, that's all."

Liam said, "Well, I certainly had nothing to do with Darren's death. I'm horrified that you could even think so. I'd gone to the office early the day Darren died, which I've already told the police." He frowned. "Does your son know you're investigating Darren's death? Isn't that supposed to be *his* job?"

Myrtle said breezily, "Red Clover appreciates my valuable insights when he's solving cases."

Miles made a strangled sound and Myrtle glared at him.

She looked directly at Liam. "Do you have any thoughts about who might have ended Darren's life? Since you were in the office and not involved?"

Liam gave her a thoughtful look. "You have to understand that anything I say is off-the-record. My name is not to be used in any way in any sort of publication. You also need to know that these are just musings, not evidence."

"Spoken as a true attorney," murmured Miles. He didn't appear to like Liam very much.

Myrtle said coolly, "Of course."

"Besides, this constitutes hearsay. Because what I'm about to tell you is from Darren's mouth. And Darren, naturally, is dead," said Liam.

Myrtle was starting to fidget. "Of course," she said again, tersely.

"What's more . . ." started Liam.

"For heaven's sake, just spit it out!" said Myrtle.

Liam looked miffed. "I was just about to get there. So, here's the thing. Darren told me his family was encroaching on him since the sale of the painting he found in the attic. They'd never asked for money before, nor indicated that they needed any. It seemed to be bothering him deeply. I advised him to put the money into investments instead of keeping it liquid."

"And that's what he did?" asked Miles.

Liam shook his head. "I don't think so. He didn't seem very interested in doing so. As he put it, he wanted the money more liquid for himself. In his view, he was an older guy and didn't have time to keep money tied up in investments for decades. So

I advised him to at least *tell his family* that he'd tied the money up. That way they'd stop bugging him for loans."

Myrtle asked, "Was Orabelle asking Darren? Or just Tripp?"

"He didn't specifically say. To me, though, 'family' is plural." He looked at his watch. "Now, I really must go. Enjoy your lunch."

And, with apparent relief, he quickly left.

Miles just as quickly moved to the other side of the booth. "It looks weird for us to be sitting next to each other with no one across from us," he said. "People will talk."

"In Bradley, it's all they seem to do anyway," said Myrtle.

"What do you make of Liam?" asked Miles as he took another bite of his salad. He hadn't made much progress with his meal while they were talking to the attorney.

Myrtle, on the other hand, had neatly polished off her food. She said, "I think he's a man with secrets. New York, my eye."

"You think he was from Boston," said Miles.

"I do. I think he has some sort of secret buried in his past and didn't want Darren digging it up."

Miles put his fork down and placed his hands on either side of his forehead.

Myrtle gave him an alarmed look. "Do you have a migraine, Miles?"

He shook his head. "I'm thinking."

"It appears to be a painful process," muttered Myrtle.

Miles said slowly, "I think I'm remembering something from one of Darren's and my chess games."

"Well, it's about time!" Myrtle leaned across the table. "What do you remember?"

"I remember Darren saying something about realizing someone wasn't exactly who they seemed." Miles stopped.

"Come on, Miles, you can do it."

He continued, "He kept saying he never forgot a face." He stopped again. "That's all I've got."

"Never forgot a face," said Myrtle thoughtfully.

Miles said, "That's right. I remember it because I admired that trait. I frequently forget faces."

"That must have been quite a hazard as a pharmaceutical salesman. I'd have thought knowing faces should have been part of your stock-in-trade."

"Engineer," grated Miles coldly. "I was an engineer."

"Whatever," said Myrtle in an airy voice.

Miles finished his salad and looked at the bill the waitress had left on the table. "How about if I get this?"

Myrtle shook her head. "I've already carefully counted out my portion of the tip and bill. I can pay most of it with spare change." She pulled a bulging change purse out.

Miles knew better than to argue with Myrtle when she'd made her mind up. They paid up at the front, with Myrtle carefully counting out what seemed to mostly be nickels and dimes, and then headed to the car and returned to Myrtle's house.

Miles cast a wary eye on the giant gnome at the front of the yard as he put the car in park. "That gnome is particularly disturbing to me somehow."

"It's because it's unnatural. Gnomes shouldn't look like that." Myrtle glanced across her yard and scowled. "You know, I don't think Dusty remembered to spray my weeds."

"It does take a while for them to curl up and die, you know. You probably won't see any results for a couple of days."

Myrtle got out of the car. "I won't see any results for longer than that because he didn't spray." She walked in her front door and out to the back. Sure enough, the weed killer was completely full and still sitting outside.

"That Dusty," she growled. "I'll have to call him and give him a piece of my mind."

"There's no point in worrying about it now. You can call him later. I'm not sure weeds could survive under all those gnomes anyway." Miles settled back on Myrtle's sofa. Myrtle settled back in her armchair and once again picked up the remote to put the soap opera on.

But the phone rang. Miles rolled his eyes as they were interrupted again. "I could use some mindless entertainment right about now," he said with a sigh.

"*Tomorrow's Promise* isn't mindless. We must think really, really hard to keep up with the convoluted storylines." Myrtle dug her cell phone out of her purse and frowned at it. "Wanda?" she asked as she answered. "Is everything all right?"

"Did you take care of them weeds?" asked Wanda.

"The weeds? No. Dusty is hopeless. I'll have to see if he can take care of it later."

"So you still have a lot of it," said Wanda.

"The weed killer? Yes, a full bottle. Now I have a question for you. We're trying to figure out more about Liam-the-lawyer. But Pansy doesn't have a lot of information and Miles doesn't listen."

Miles sighed again from the sofa.

Wanda said, "Them newspapers was important."

Myrtle knit her brows. "The ones Darren found in his attic? That reminded him of Liam's past?"

"Them very ones."

Myrtle said, "All right, but the newspapers are gone now. And Pansy was very vague about the time period involved. She mentioned hurricanes or blizzards or something."

"Try a blizzard."

"All right. I'll look online."

Wanda said, "One more thing. Might want to check yer funeral clothes."

"I will most certainly be doing that because I intend to be attending a funeral in a couple of days. Darren's. I keep making the dumb mistake of not checking my funeral outfit and then finding a spot where I spilled on it from the last funeral. You'd think if I wore a garment for only two hours, it would be spot-free."

"Just sayin' you might want to check it now." Wanda paused. "That is all." There was a click and she was gone.

Miles said dryly, "More cryptic messages from Wanda?"

"Yes. More about the weed killer. And I'm to look up a blizzard online, and check my funeral outfit."

Miles said, "Are any of them for immediate action? Because I'd like to watch the soap finally."

Myrtle strode toward her bedroom, calling behind her, "Just the one. This will only take a minute."

But it seemed to take slightly longer than a minute and Miles fidgeted on the sofa. Myrtle finally came back, bearing the two-piece funeral outfit in her hands. "Miles, *you* take a look.

Wanda told me to check out my outfit. I don't see a single spot on it. There don't seem to be any missing buttons. The zipper is fully functional." Myrtle demonstrated the zipper's abilities and flipped the outfit around so that Miles could view both the front and back of the garments.

Miles said, "Have you checked the pockets?"

Myrtle put her hand into one of the pockets and pulled out cash. "Money!" she said, holding her hand aloft and grinning at the bills.

"How much?"

"More than I had before," said Myrtle contentedly. She swiftly counted it. "Twenty-five dollars."

"Cash seems an odd thing to find in your funeral attire," observed Miles.

Myrtle nodded. "Yes. I'd never have thought to look there if dear Wanda hadn't advised me to. Of course, I'd have come across it in a couple of days for Darren's funeral, but she's absolutely right that it's needed *today*." She frowned thoughtfully. "You know, this must have been at Sarah Denver's funeral. Evaline Michaels gave me money to pay me back for the food I brought for the reception."

Miles raised his eyebrows. "You brought that much food?"

"I did. Evaline put in an order for deli sandwich and fruit and cheese platters from the Piggly Wiggly and then was unable to come pick them up because she had a ghastly cold. I picked them up for her and she paid me back. Elaine drove me to the store and the funeral reception and helped me carry everything and I paid for it all."

"That seems like a lot of food for Evaline to purchase," said Miles.

Myrtle shrugged. "It was on behalf of her church circle. *Anyway*, the point is that I have money now."

"That's good. Do you want me to take you back to the grocery store? With a list this time? That way you don't have to have an uncomfortable supper with Red tonight."

"Oh, I'm looking forward to my uncomfortable supper. That's when I hope to end up with more information. No, I'm just going to use a little bit at a time of my unexpected windfall." She carefully put the money in her wallet.

Miles was relieved to see Myrtle settle back into her chair and finally pick up the remote. He gave a contented sigh as the soap opera started playing.

Chapter Twelve

After Miles returned home, Pasha was fed, and Dusty fussed at, Myrtle trotted across the street to Red and Elaine's house. She had to wait for a slow-moving car to pass before she crossed. The occupants all appeared to be taking pictures of her gnomes. Or, perhaps, they were zooming in on the giant gnome, quite the anomaly in the group. Myrtle preened, managing to photobomb their pictures.

A few minutes later, Elaine pulled up an extra chair to the kitchen table and set a big plate of spaghetti in front of Myrtle.

The entertainment for the evening was Jack. He was apparently a tremendous fan of spaghetti and was enthusiastically shoveling it into his mouth. However, his expertise with his little-kid-sized fork was clearly lacking. Plus, he kept grinning at the novelty of seeing his Nana at the table with them and then missing his mouth altogether.

Red was very occupied with cleaning off Jack's face after his near-misses and complete-and-total-misses.

Myrtle raised her eyebrows at this. "Isn't that a waste of time until the end of supper?"

"He doesn't want his face messy," said Red.

Myrtle suspected that Jack cared a lot less about the condition of his face than Red did.

"More bread, Myrtle?" asked Elaine. "Oh, and I want you to try a new dessert I worked on this afternoon. I'm pretty excited about it. It's a cranberry-apple lattice pie."

Myrtle beamed at her. "I would *love* to try it." This, in Myrtle's mind, was Elaine's best hobby ever.

She turned her attention on Red, who was still distracted by removing red sauce from Jack. "How is the case going, Red?"

Red grunted. "Okay, I guess."

"Did any neighbors happen to see anyone leaving Darren's house that morning? Or have you figured out what the motive behind the murder was?" asked Myrtle innocently. Red was never very forthcoming, but she hoped he was preoccupied enough to answer.

He clearly wasn't. "Keep out of the case, Mama." He straightened back up, looking pleased at his handiwork. Jack gave him a grin and stuffed another handful of spaghetti onto his cheek.

Elaine gave Myrtle an apologetic look.

Myrtle said, "Red, I've actually been able, though sources, to find out very interesting information on this case."

Now his attention was fully-focused on his mother. "What kind of interesting information?"

"Information about Liam."

Red scowled at her. "Darren's attorney? What about him?"

Myrtle shrugged. "Oh, I don't know. Seems like if I give you helpful information, you should compensate me with a fair trade. With helpful information that *you've* obtained."

Red sighed. "You know I don't talk about police business, Mama. Besides, I don't even know if what you've discovered is all that helpful."

"I just want to know if there's a clear motive."

Red shook his head. "I'm not answering that."

"Okay, how about this—did any of Darren's neighbors happen to see anything when Darren was killed? People should have been out and about. I'd think somebody would have spotted a murderer skulking around in Darren's boxwoods."

Red swiped at Jack's mouth again. "Okay. I'll disclose that information, but only because I don't want you to go knocking on Darren's neighbors' doors and harassing them. No, nobody saw anything. On the one side, they'd all headed off to work. On the other side, they were checking emails and responding to them and totally focused on their computer. So there was nothing helpful at all." He turned his attention on Myrtle. "Now on to your interesting information."

Myrtle smiled smugly, enjoying the spotlight. "Well, I was speaking with Wanda."

Red help up a hand. "Let me stop you right there."

Elaine said, "Red, be polite."

Red rubbed his face with his hands, forgetting the napkin he'd been using to swab Jack's face was still in one hand. A glob of spaghetti sauce transferred to his cheek.

Myrtle frowned at the spaghetti sauce and at Red. "Really, Red, I'm disappointed in you. It seems you don't really pay attention. Wanda is gifted. You've seen that in other cases."

Red held up his hand as if warding off more talk of the psychic. "I don't know what I've seen, Mama."

Myrtle sighed. "All right, then. Let me start at this from another angle. *Pansy* also told me about Liam. It seems Liam and Darren might not have been getting along."

"I'm a little confused about why they might need to get along at all. They're not married to each other. They're not friends. They were just attorney and client."

Myrtle said, "Except Darren thought Liam might not have been exactly what he seemed."

"Really?" Now Red looked as if he might be paying attention. Jack grinned joyfully at his grandmother and inaccurately stuffed spaghetti at his face again.

"Really. It seems Darren might have recognized Liam from his days living in Boston."

Red said, "I thought Liam was from New York."

"Well, that's what he wants us all to believe. But have you ever heard a New York accent like that?"

Red looked thoughtful. "No. Although I don't hear a lot of New York accents on a daily basis, except on TV."

Myrtle gave a satisfied bob of her head. "Exactly. Now, the trouble is that we don't really know what the time period was. Pansy said Darren mentioned some sort of natural disaster in Boston at the time: a blizzard or a hurricane or some such."

Red said, "It's not a lot to go on, but I'll give it to the state police. They have more people and resources to handle a search like that." He grudgingly added, "Thanks, Mama."

Myrtle beamed at him and at Jack, who was now covered with spaghetti and sauce again.

Elaine took away the plates and said, "Does anyone want pie? We also have pie. Here, I'll just put a few options and plates out." She glanced at Jack and laughed. "But first, I'll clean Jack up. In the bathroom this time, I think. It looks like it's even in his hair somehow."

She whisked Jack away and Red sighed and patted his tummy. "My girth is the only problem with this new hobby of Elaine's. Pies, cakes, breads, pastries. I'm gaining weight like crazy."

Myrtle said, "Actually, the extra pounds don't look bad on you. You were always too thin as a boy."

"That's definitely not the problem anymore," said Red with a moan. "Just wait. You'll see if you keep coming over here, you're going to start gaining, too. It's impossible not to."

"I usually stay precisely the same weight," said Myrtle proudly. "I'm already big-boned. I'm not *thin*, but I don't really gain. Maybe it's a side effect of being in one's eighties."

Red looked doubtful. "If you say so, Mama." He reached in his pocket and pulled out his wallet. "I wanted to give you a little something just to tide you over until the end of the week."

Myrtle shook her head. "I don't need a loan."

"Not a loan. A gift. You've certainly helped me out in the past. Consider it repayment." He held out a few twenties.

Myrtle said firmly, "No. No, thank you, Red. I actually discovered some money in an outfit of mine and I won't need anything now."

He raised his eyebrows and put the money back in his wallet. "So you didn't *have* to have supper with us tonight?"

"Of course I did. You're my family and I wanted to visit. And don't worry—I won't gain an ounce."

But unfortunately, two days later and back at her own home, Myrtle was putting on her funeral outfit for Darren's service and found it to be a bit snug. She sighed and found some slacks that ran large and a top that was slightly big. Myrtle was alarmed to see how well both items now fit.

The doorbell rang and Myrtle hurried over to open it. Miles stared at her. "You're not wearing your funeral outfit."

Myrtle made a face. "It doesn't fit very well today."

Miles said, "That must be contagious. My suit pants were too tight this morning so I had to wear something else. But I'm going to take care of the problem."

Myrtle found her purse. "You're going to get the pants altered?"

"No. I'm going to exercise and eat salads and not eat more of Elaine's baking. I think the book club food did me in. And Bo's Diner likely didn't help." Miles gave his tummy a miserable look.

"Just think if you'd had supper with her a couple of days ago, like I did. She had all sorts of pies and other stuff. This hobby, as innocent as it seemed, is now just as dangerous as all her other hobbies." Myrtle closed and locked the door behind her as she and Miles headed to his car.

There was a rather brisk wind at the cemetery, which was doing a number on Myrtle's hair. It stood up on end and she tried in vain to tamp it back down, sighing as she did. There were a fair number of people at the service, but then Darren had been a long-time resident of Bradley. It became even more well-attended after it started, with other mourners gathering.

Miles murmured to Myrtle, "I'm surprised Carter Radnor is here. We keep hearing how he and Darren were at odds."

"Yes, but you can see where he's looking."

Miles raised his eyebrows. "Right over at Pansy."

"Just like a lovesick puppy," muttered Myrtle.

Pansy, for her part, was looking very much like the grieving girlfriend. She wasn't seated on the front row by the grave like Orabelle, Tripp, and other family members, but was seated in the row behind them. However, she certainly made her presence known with the occasional loud sob.

The service went like clockwork. Myrtle figured Orabelle, who generally ran things like a drill sergeant, was behind the planning and execution of the event. There was a short, simple homily, a soloist with a single hymn, and a reading of Psalm 23. Then it was over and Orabelle invited everyone to the church hall.

Myrtle and Miles climbed back into his car to head to the church. "There's going to be quite a spread," said Myrtle. "Orabelle is very involved in the church."

"And Darren wasn't a slacker either," said Miles. "I believe he went to church every week for Bible study."

"There's going to be a *lot* of food," said Myrtle. "And I'm sure Carter will be there. After all, he's living on his own. There's absolutely no way he's going to turn down the opportunity of free Southern food cooked by the loving and experienced hands of an army of church ladies."

As Myrtle had predicted, the tables in the church hall were absolutely laden with food and the church ladies had truly outdone themselves. There were deviled eggs, sandwiches of every kind and variety, fried chicken, potato salad, ham in homemade biscuits, and a variety of other mouthwatering stuff.

"Come on, let's load up plates before we scout out Carter," said Myrtle.

Plates piled high, they looked for a spot to sit down and found a couple of chairs near the beverage table (also weighed down, but with iced tea, lemonade, punch, and other drinks).

Miles looked thoughtfully around the room. "I haven't seen Carter yet."

"Look for Pansy," muttered Myrtle as she took another big bite of baked macaroni and cheese.

Sure enough, as soon as they spotted Pansy, they saw Carter hovering nearby.

Miles knit his brows. "I can't say I approve of Carter's behavior. It's a hair away from stalking, isn't it? I can't imagine that Pansy appreciates the way he's acting. She's grieving for Darren, for pity's sake."

Myrtle studied the scene for a minute. "I think she's very *aware* of him. I'm not sure she's bothered by him, though."

"It's Darren's funeral," said Miles, miffed on Darren's behalf.

"Then let's break up his little reverie on Pansy," said Myrtle, putting down her fork and heading toward Carter with Miles following.

Myrtle gave a theatrical stumble very close to Carter and he automatically, and quite chivalrously, grabbed her by the arm and prevented her from falling. He should, perhaps, have wondered why Myrtle didn't simply catch herself with her cane, but he appeared to be a man of limited imagination.

Chapter Thirteen

"Gracious," said Myrtle. "Thank you, Carter. I seem to be a bit unsteady today."

A frowning figure in the background caught her eye and she sighed as she realized Red spotted her stumble. He would either think it evidence that she needed to be driven straight to Greener Pastures retirement home or else he would think she was pumping Carter for information. Neither was good.

"That's no problem at all, Myrtle," said Carter politely, his attention again straying to Pansy.

Miles was hanging back and Myrtle pulled him forward. "You remember Miles, of course."

Carter gave him a smile. "How are you, Miles?"

Miles was still steamed about the lack of respect shown Darren. He pointedly said, "Oh, I suppose I'm all right. Although I'm very sorry about Darren. He was a great guy."

Carter frowned. "Somehow I didn't realize you two knew each other that well."

"We played chess together regularly," said Miles stiffly.

"I see. I've never been much of a chess guy, myself."

"I suppose not." Miles gave him a cold look.

A cloud passed over Carter's features as if he wasn't quite sure if his intelligence was being besmirched or not.

Myrtle stepped in before Miles became even more antagonistic. "Miles and I were actually the ones who discovered poor Darren. It was a terrible morning."

Carter lifted his eyebrows. "I didn't realize that. I'm sorry. I wish I'd known Darren needed help. I was at home with Crystal."

"Crystal?" Myrtle knit her eyebrows.

"My dog. He's a real lap dog. Loves to sit in my lap in the mornings when I'm reading the paper," said Carter.

Myrtle curled her lip a little. "I see. You know, I have a cat named Pasha. She's decidedly *not* a lap cat. She's absolutely brilliant and a master hunter. You'd be amazed to hear the types of prey she's brought in."

Carter was apparently never one to back away from a competition. "I didn't mean to imply that Crystal *wasn't* a hunter. He's a terrier mix and has brought in some fine catches, himself."

"Bats," said Myrtle.

"Chipmunks," said Carter.

"Rabbits."

Carter's eyes narrowed. "Squirrels."

"Snakes."

Carter opened his mouth and Miles, looking queasy, stepped in. "Can we perhaps not talk about this now?"

"Poor Miles doesn't have the stomach for gore," said Myrtle affectionately. Then she cut right to the chase. "You know, I didn't realize that *you* knew Darren so well, Carter."

Carter stuttered a little. "I didn't, I suppose. Not as well as the two of you, anyway."

Myrtle raised her eyebrows. "Then it's very charitable of you to attend his funeral. I know you must be a very busy man . . . owning your own insurance business and whatnot."

Miles shifted uncomfortably from foot to foot at the mention of Carter's vocation. He did not want to be sold any insurance.

Carter mumbled, "I suppose I wanted to be here to support Pansy."

"That's very nice. Although it looks as if Pansy has lots of support."

They glanced over at Pansy, surrounded by a sympathetic gaggle of women.

"Funnily enough, Carter, although you didn't know Darren well, someone mentioned you'd argued with him recently." Myrtle smiled innocently at Carter.

Carter's eyes grew huge, then narrowed suspiciously. "Wait, you write for the newspaper, don't you?"

Myrtle puffed with pride. She always liked when this fact was recognized. "Yes, I do. I'm a crime reporter there, as a matter of fact."

Miles sighed. Myrtle so frequently avoided the unpleasant fact that she usually wrote the paper's helpful hints column.

"However, this is off-the-record, of course."

Carter said, "Well, maybe you can set the record straight with whoever you heard that from. Yes, I had words with Darren. But that's only because Pansy called me in tears. It made me

see red that he'd not been treating Pansy the way she deserved."
His hands pulled into fists at the memory.

Myrtle asked, "Pansy and Darren had been arguing?"

"That's right. Darren wasn't a saint, you know. Despite the
fact that he's gone now." He said the last words with satisfaction.

"Why did they argue?" asked Miles.

Carter seemed to realize he might be making Pansy more
of a suspect. He hastily said, "It wasn't much of an argument
on Pansy's side, according to her. She said Darren just suddenly
seemed to snap and was raging at her."

"Not physically?" asked Myrtle with a frown.

Even Carter wasn't willing to go that far. "No," he muttered.
"He just yelled at her. But she's not used to being yelled at. I
didn't ask her what it was about because it was none of my business. All I know is that she's always been devoted to Darren and
he obviously didn't realize what a treasure he had in Pansy. He
should have appreciated her more. And he sure shouldn't have
been yelling at her like that. Anyway, I went over to give Darren
a piece of my mind."

Myrtle raised an eyebrow. "And when you finished giving
him that piece of your mind, he was still alive?"

"Alive and kicking," said Carter. His gaze, as if drawn by a
magnet, sought out Pansy. He looked troubled as a handsome
widower in town started engaging in conversation with her.
"Look, I need to go."

"Nice talking to you," said Myrtle sweetly to Carter's back as
he abruptly left.

Miles said, "Good riddance. He shouldn't be at a funeral if
he's not grieving."

Myrtle said, "How peevish of you, Miles. I'd say there were plenty of people here who don't appear to be grieving." She frowned at Erma Sherman, her annoying neighbor, who was currently giving a braying laugh at something she'd just said to someone else. Then her gaze flitted over to someone else. "Actually, I'd say Tripp wasn't looking too upset about his uncle's demise."

They sat down in a couple of folding chairs to observe. Miles said charitably, "It could be a lack of sleep."

Myrtle muttered. "Or too much alcohol."

"Grief?" offered Miles, still trying to see Darren's family in a positive light.

"Or drugs," countered Myrtle.

Miles got them another plate of food since the church ladies continued restocking it and bringing out fresh options. Myrtle said, "At this rate, I won't have to eat supper tonight."

Miles said, "There's so much food that Orabelle and Tripp are going to be eating out of their freezers for months." He glanced around the room. "Where did Carter go? This time I don't see him around Pansy. Did he give up and leave?"

"He certainly should have if he hasn't. Pansy is clearly being charmed by Marcus Washington," said Myrtle dryly. She watched as Pansy beamed up at him and he beamed back.

Miles said, "Oh, there he is." He paused. "Wait, is that . . . ?"

"It's Orabelle. And she's actually *smiling* for once."

Miles said, "And at Carter."

Myrtle and Miles observed silently while they munched on ham biscuits.

Myrtle said, "I must say, I think Orabelle and Carter would be a far better match than Carter and Pansy. Pansy has way too much baggage."

"Well, all three of them are murder suspects, so I'd say they all have a bit of baggage."

Myrtle said, "True. But at least Orabelle is sensible. Pansy is too flighty for my tastes." She paused. "It looks as if Carter might be at least somewhat receptive."

"He's not looking longingly at Pansy right now, anyway," agreed Miles.

"Oh goodness, here comes Red," said Myrtle with a sigh. "What does he want?"

"Likely to fuss at you for questioning Carter." Miles took his glasses off and solemnly wiped them. "I think I'll go speak with . . . someone." He quickly walked away.

Red said, "Hi, Mama." He raised his eyebrows. "I do believe you're not wearing your usual funeral outfit."

Myrtle said crossly, "Smarty-pants. The slacks didn't fit very well, so I had to improvise."

Lieutenant Perkins came over to join them and Myrtle gave him a big smile. He said politely, "I thought I might see you here. I wanted to give you this." He reached into his suit pocket and pulled out a small book of crosswords. Perkins hesitated and then said, "My mother is also a big crossword puzzle fan and she recommended this collection. It's supposed to be pretty challenging."

Myrtle beamed at him. "Isn't that so thoughtful?" She turned to Red and gave him a pointed look. "Don't you think that's so thoughtful, Red? A gift! And just because he and his mother thought I might enjoy it."

Red sighed. Clearly, Lieutenant Perkins was racking up more points in the area of thoughtfulness than he was. He said grudgingly, "That's very nice."

Perkins smiled back at Myrtle. "As soon as my mother mentioned the book, I thought of you."

"And I'll get started on it right away. The puzzles in our paper are quite rudimentary. To make them more challenging, I set a timer for myself and try to beat my best time."

Red muttered under his breath, "Some people need less time on their hands."

Myrtle narrowed her eyes at him.

"By the way, Mama, why were you speaking with Carter Radnor?" Red's eyes narrowed suspiciously.

Myrtle said innocently, "Why, because he was *there*. Is there something I should *know* about Carter Radnor? He's not a person of interest in your case, is he?"

Red immediately looked as if he regretted saying anything at all.

Perkins said, "We should probably be heading out now."

Myrtle turned again to Perkins and said, "Thanks so much again."

Miles and Myrtle stayed for a little while longer at the funeral reception before leaving to head back to Myrtle's house.

"What's next on the agenda?" asked Miles.

Myrtle said, "I have to write up a piece for the paper."

Miles asked, "On the funeral?"

Myrtle made a face. "For that helpful hints column. I wish Sloan would cancel it, but it still seems wildly popular. Anyway, I'm supposed to send that in this afternoon. And then I think I'll mull all this over. The suspects, the crime. Maybe I can think of what direction we need to head in next."

Miles looked relieved. "That sounds good. I was actually hoping for some downtime. I have a few things I need to do around the house."

Myrtle raised an eyebrow. "That sounds intriguing. What sorts of things?"

"I need to weed out some of my older khakis in my closet and retire them as yard clothes, for one."

"Sounds like an exciting afternoon," said Myrtle dryly.

"Not exciting, but helpful. I keep accidentally pulling out old pairs of khakis and not realizing they're the frayed ones until later. This will end up saving me time." Miles sounded as if he was warming to his topic and Myrtle worried he might continue with a dissertation on organizing his sock drawer.

She quickly jumped in, "That's all very productive of you, Miles. Thanks for the ride to the funeral. Talk to you later?" And she hurried out of the car.

The helpful hints column took a bit longer than planned when she couldn't find the tip Penny Holcomb had sent in. Penny was the kind of person who'd hound her about it every time she saw Myrtle. She swore the woman had some sort of a chip on her shoulder. And Myrtle couldn't for the life of her remember *what* the tip was, only that Penny had been the one to submit it.

Pasha watched Myrtle with interest as Myrtle tore through her desk, un-tidying the very tidy drawers, nooks and crannies.

Then she attacked her recycling bin, checking to see if she'd accidentally flung the bit of paper out with her old magazines and newspapers.

After far too much time had gone by, Myrtle gave up and opened up her Word program. Then she stared at the computer. Apparently, she'd been so very organized that she'd put Penny's tip in her column and then tossed out the piece of paper.

Frustrated by her own efficiency, Myrtle finished writing the column, sent it to Sloan, and then set about cleaning up the mess she'd made. By the time she'd finished, she wandered back to her computer. Perhaps now was the perfect time to find out more about the lawyer, Liam Hudson, and his mysterious past.

After fifteen or twenty minutes and numerous online rabbit holes to fall down, Myrtle realized it wasn't going to be as easy as it seemed. But she had discovered one very interesting thing: Liam didn't appear to have an online past. Anything about Liam online originated about ten years ago here in Bradley. That seemed rather odd. Myrtle herself had more of an online profile than that and it dated back further.

So perhaps Liam changed his name at some point to escape his past. Myrtle decided it might be more fruitful to focus on natural disasters in the Boston area. Pansy hadn't been at all convincing that it was a hurricane, so Myrtle broadened her search.

After some time, Myrtle sighed. Apparently, Boston had been afflicted by any number of things. She was about to give up when she saw mention of a blizzard that was around the same time period. Myrtle pulled up the archived paper for every mention of the blizzard and glanced through them—until she saw a photo of a young man with a couple of other young men who appeared to be a very scruffy version of Liam.

She quickly read the article. It seemed Liam, or Jeremy, as the paper called him, had unsavory friends at the time and drove the getaway car when his friends robbed a convenience store . . . and shot the store clerk. Was Liam in the wrong place at the wrong time with the wrong people or was he an accessory?

Armed with his original name, Myrtle searched for more information. It seemed a jury had decided Liam was guilty, but because it was a first offense for the young man, the judge had only awarded him community service and time served. This had apparently made the family of the murdered store clerk furious. No wonder he'd changed his name.

She heard talking outside and checked out her window. Red was talking on his phone, rather loudly in her way of thinking, while getting into his police cruiser.

Myrtle called Miles. "Want to follow Red on a call?"

Miles sounded dubious. "Do I? Aren't Red's calls usually to do with neighbor disputes and children trespassing on lawns?"

"Usually so, but this time I think he might have been phoned about something important. Let's find out."

A couple of minutes later, Miles pulled up in Myrtle's driveway. By this time, however, Red was already gone.

Myrtle said impatiently, "He headed in the direction of downtown Bradley. Let's see if we can find him."

Miles obediently put the car in gear and backed carefully down the driveway and out on the street.

"Pick up the pace a little or we'll never find him."

Miles muttered, "You've watched too many car chases on TV. Besides, this is a very small town. I think we'll be able to find him."

A minute later, Myrtle said abruptly, "Stop the car. I see Red."

Miles pulled to the side of the road. "Is something happening at the diner?"

"No, I think he's going *behind* the diner. To the back of the office building." Myrtle leaned closer to the window and made a disgusted sound. "No, it's too dark. I can't see a thing. You'd think we'd have street lights out here. Let's get out of the car."

"Red's not going to like this," said Miles gloomily.

"We're going to tell him we happened to be driving by." Myrtle was already getting out of the car.

"Isn't that a little suspicious? That's not ordinarily what we do."

Myrtle said, "We'll just say we were bored and decided to go for a little drive. He won't care—he's clearly going to be all wrapped up with whatever he's working on."

Fortunately, the back of the brick office building next to the diner was illuminated by Red's headlights. As they approached, they could see Red speaking with Tripp Whitley.

"What's that on the ground?" asked Miles in a halting voice.

Myrtle said, "Let's get a little closer."

Miles trailed behind her unhappily.

"I do believe it might be a body," said Myrtle thoughtfully.

Chapter Fourteen

Red spotted his mother coming and held up a hand to Tripp before stalking over.

"Mama, what on earth are you doing here?" he hissed.

"Oh, Miles and I were just driving by and we saw your car." Myrtle paused. "Is that Liam Hudson?"

Red's eyes were suspicious. "How exactly did you know that?"

"A simple deduction. His office is directly above the spot on the pavement where I see a body," said Myrtle coolly.

Red rubbed his face. "I don't have time for this. I need to block off the area, speak with Tripp, and get the state police over here."

Myrtle nodded her head. "Don't worry. Miles and I will stay right here."

"Mama, I don't *want* you to stay right here. I want you to continue on your little nocturnal drive or get your late-night ice cream snack or head back home. I want you anywhere *but* here." Red was starting to get agitated.

Miles said, "Come on Myrtle, let's go."

Myrtle said, "What you don't know, Red, is that I have some very important information that you're going to want to hear. So I'll stay put."

"Whatever you think you know, I can hear it tomorrow." Red was already pulling his cell phone out of his pocket.

"Fine," said Myrtle complacently. "I'll wait to speak with Lieutenant Perkins. He'll want to hear all about what I've discovered about Liam Hudson."

Red's eyes narrowed. "What exactly . . . never mind. Okay, wait here, but know it might take some time."

"We'll be just fine," said Myrtle with a sniff. Red stomped away, now speaking with the state police on the phone as he returned to his police cruiser and pulled out crime scene tape.

Miles said, "I do have some folding chairs in my trunk. I could pull them out for us."

"Perfect," said Myrtle. "That way we don't have to go all the way back to the car."

Miles retrieved the chairs and set them up out of the way of the crime scene tape, but close enough so that they could see what was going on. They watched as Red finished speaking with Tripp and then seemed to dismiss him after the state police finally drove up. He talked to them for a while and then walked over to where Miles and Myrtle sat in their chairs.

"What did you find out?" asked Red.

"Interestingly enough, Liam Hudson wasn't exactly who he said he was."

"He wasn't a lawyer?" Miles blinked.

"Oh, I'm sure he must have a law degree. But he didn't originally start out as Liam Hudson. He changed his name, most likely because of a legal issue he encountered in Boston when he was a young man hanging out with a rough crowd."

Red frowned. "He got into trouble?"

"He did indeed. Although not as much trouble as he could have gotten into—a local judge was apparently quite lenient with him. Or merciful or something. Anyway, the family of the store clerk who was shot and killed wasn't very pleased with the sentencing. I'm guessing Liam was trying to escape his past with his name change and the move here. And, for the most part, I suppose he did."

"And then Darren somehow remembered who he was," said Red.

"Apparently, there were newspapers Darren kept because of a historic blizzard that had happened while he was living in Boston. I suppose, with the discovery of the painting, Darren decided to spend some more time rooting around in his attic to see what else he might be able to find. He opened up the newspapers and noticed something that had previously escaped his attention." Myrtle shrugged.

Red's eyes narrowed. "This all makes a lot of sense except for one thing. Liam is dead. It seems to me that if he'd killed Darren to keep him quiet and protect his law business, Liam would still be alive and well."

Miles cleared his throat. "Was it . . . well, did Liam jump?"

Red hesitated. Then he said, "It doesn't look that way, actually. There's some evidence to suggest otherwise. That's what's so confusing about the situation. Besides, I don't think Liam would have wanted to kill himself anyway, even if he'd killed Darren. The whole *point* of murdering Darren would have been to ensure that Liam's life continued on as normal." He glanced over as Lieutenant Perkins arrived on the scene. "Let me go talk with Perkins. I need to get the state police on Liam's history pronto."

He hurried away and Myrtle sang out, "You're welcome!"

Miles said, "Well, we should go then, shouldn't we? You've spoken with Red. We found out Liam was murdered. We should leave and get out of their way."

"Except we're not *in* their way. And Tripp is coming over. Don't you want to find out how he figures into the equation?"

Miles's expression stated that he wasn't sure that was really at all necessary but he reluctantly stayed seated.

Tripp greeted them and said, a hint of mockery in his voice, "Is this what passes as evening entertainment in Bradley?"

Miles flushed, but Myrtle said smoothly, "Don't be silly, Tripp. We were waiting to speak with Red and provide him with some useful information, which we just did. As I suppose you did, yourself?"

Tripp nodded. "Yeah. I was back here meeting someone and saw something on the ground." His face, even in the darkness, looked pale.

Meeting someone back here at this time of night didn't exactly sound like aboveboard business, but Myrtle was willing to let that slide. "I see. And you called the police. But you didn't see what happened before that?"

He shook his head. "No. But I saw it wasn't any suicide. The guy had marks on the inner part of his upper arms. It looked like he was grabbed and shoved."

Miles said slowly, "Isn't it also unusual for suicides to take place at one's workplace?"

Myrtle said, "I suppose, except this is the tallest building in Bradley, so if defenestration were on one's mind, that might make a difference. But it sounds as if Red agreed with you, Tripp—that this was murder."

"Can I smoke?" asked Tripp suddenly. He pulled a pack of cigarettes out of his pocket without waiting for an answer.

Myrtle said sternly, "As long as you don't blow the smoke in our direction. We're seniors. We have delicate lungs."

Tripp seemed altogether more jittery than was required, even considering the occasion. His eyes were bloodshot, too. Myrtle suspected he had something more potent than nicotine coursing through his body. "Are you finished speaking with the police? Can we give you a lift home?"

Tripp nodded, took a few more drags on his cigarette and then stomped it out. After seeing Myrtle's expression, he carefully picked it up off the ground and stuck it in his pocket instead of littering. "Yeah, they're done with me. A ride home would be great. I walked over here but I'd rather not walk back."

They all climbed into Miles's car.

Myrtle said, "So you were meeting someone out here?" Her tone seemed to suggest that this was an odd thing to do at that particular location.

Tripp said wryly, "Believe me, your son has already given me a hard time about what my business was out there. You're a straight-shooter, Miss Myrtle, so I'll call it what it is: addiction. I have an issue and I was out there trying to feed my habit. It was obviously a really crummy idea since I immediately came across a body."

Miles said, "What did Red say?"

"Oh, he wasn't really amused by the whole thing. But I gotta say, he's generous, Miss M. Red said he was willing to look the other way on the drug stuff as long as I got cleaned up. Even emailed me a list of resources from his phone."

Myrtle raised her eyebrows. "Good for him. I wasn't sure what he'd do in that case."

"I guess he was more worried about the body than anything else, so maybe it was good timing for me. But he did say he can't have any drug activity in Bradley, so this was my one and only chance," said Tripp. "Of course, he said I'm still considered a suspect in my uncle's death and to let him know if I end up leaving town."

Myrtle said, "Have you had any other ideas about what might have happened to your uncle? And do you think what happened might have been somehow motivated by the money he made from the sale of that painting?"

Tripp snorted. "A straight-shooter, just like I figured. To answer your question, I have no clue what happened to him. But yeah, money is a real motivator. Even my mom asked Darren for money."

This prompted Myrtle to turn around to look at Tripp in the back seat. "Did she?"

"That surprises you," noted Tripp with a sly smile.

"Well, she always seems so content. So competent."

Tripp said, "She can be both of those things. You'd never realize she was a dreamer. At least, you wouldn't until you saw her magazine subscriptions. And the artwork in the house. Oh, and the shows she watches on TV."

"What are those?" asked Miles.

"Travel-related," said Myrtle slowly.

Tripp looked impressed. "You're a real detective."

"I simply happened to notice the art on her walls, although I didn't think a lot of it at the time. Prints of London. The Eiffel Tower. Things like that."

"Exactly," said Tripp. "Her dream is to go abroad. And funnily enough, she's never even made it out of Bradley."

"And so she asked her brother for money," said Myrtle.

"And he wouldn't give it to her. He said it was all tied up in investments and stuff. She was too proud to push him on it." Tripp shrugged. "But can you imagine my mother killing Darren in his attic?"

Myrtle actually could. Not only did she have quite a remarkable imagination, she also remembered Orabelle's steely strength.

Myrtle said, "Were you really home the morning Darren was found?"

Tripp said, "Like mother, like son. Red's already pegged me on that. No, I was off being a dope, as usual. I just made it home at sunrise."

Miles sounded startled. "There are places to go in Bradley where you can stay out all night?"

Tripp chuckled. "No, there aren't. I'd left town and come back. Anyway, I had a brilliant idea." He snorted. "At least, it seemed like a brilliant idea when I was high. I asked Darren for money. Like I said, he very politely refused me and there was no trouble. He was definitely alive and happily watering his azalea bushes when I left him."

Myrtle nodded. "And did you see anything out of the ordinary when you found Liam? Anyone lurking around in the shadows?"

Tripp shook his head. "Nope. Didn't even see the guy I was there to meet lurking around. He spotted a dead body and took off."

Miles said, "I suppose there was no motive for him to push Liam out of a window."

Tripp gave a short laugh. "He's not the kind of guy who hangs out with lawyers unless he's headed to jail. He was just here to meet with me, like I said. I gave Red his name and contact info, so he'll be checking him out, anyway. But no, it's got to be somebody else." He paused. "Red said he was Uncle Darren's lawyer. We haven't even gotten to the will and testament stage of things, so I didn't know. It seems like kind of a big coincidence that he's dead now, too."

It seemed that way to Myrtle, too. Miles pulled into Orabelle's driveway and Tripp said, "Okay, well, thanks for the ride. Good seeing the two of you." The last was said somewhat unconvincingly, but still in the same chipper voice. He hopped out of the car and disappeared inside.

Miles drove them to Myrtle's house. "If it's okay with you," he said, "I'm feeling tired. I'm going to try to get some sleep."

Myrtle nodded. "My mind is still running a million miles an hour, so I won't be doing that. I'm going to try some of Lieutenant Perkins's crosswords to wind down a little. And write an article on Liam's death for Sloan. It's too late for it to run tomorrow, but it'll make the next day's paper. And we should check in with our suspects again, starting with Pansy."

Miles raised his eyebrows. "How do you propose we do that in a natural way? You're hardly one who hangs out with Pansy on a regular basis."

"Yes, I think Pansy's a little silly sometimes. Here's the problem with Pansy: her silliness is pretend."

"You don't think she's actually silly?"

"Not a bit. When she speaks directly to me, she's a perfectly logical, intelligent-sounding human being, at least for the most part. But I've witnessed her behaving completely differently with Darren and Carter. She thinks the silliness is some sort of gambit to be appealing to men. Such a misguided approach. It's most annoying. Men like smart women," said Myrtle viciously.

Miles gave her a wary look. Myrtle was a smart woman who could occasionally be dangerous. Finally Myrtle managed to shake off her general irritation about Pansy's silliness or lack of it.

"Anyway, we'll simply pop by to say we were in the neighborhood and so happy to have her join book club. Does she have any questions for us? And how is she doing? You know, that sort of thing. We'll be *friendly*," said Myrtle, trying the word out on her tongue as if it were an exotic food.

"How early will this drop-by be?" asked Miles, wary once again.

"Oh, not early at all. A perfectly decent time. Nine o'clock."

Miles nodded. "Right."

"And we'll bring by some of Elaine's baked goods for Pansy's breakfast," said Myrtle, warming to the topic.

"Won't that negate the idea that we just happened to be in the neighborhood?"

"No, we'll say Elaine gave them to us, we had extra, and we had the brilliant idea to bring it by. See how everything falls into place?" Myrtle sounded pleased. She opened the car door and stepped outside.

"See you tomorrow," said Miles.

Myrtle wrote the piece for Sloan and emailed it off. Then she worked on one of Perkins's crosswords and found, to her delight, that it was indeed quite tricky. She had to put a good deal of thought into the process, which entertained her to no end. By the time she finished, she found to her surprise that it was one in the morning.

Also to her surprise, she heard a tap at her door. She frowned, picked up her cane, held it up threateningly, and crept to the front door. Peering out, she saw Erma Sherman with her goofy grin. Even worse, Erma appeared to be in a robe and slippers, which Myrtle decidedly didn't want to witness.

"Erma, I was just about to turn in," called Myrtle through the door.

"I won't be long," sang out Erma. "I want to talk to you about the case."

Myrtle sighed. She never liked feeling conflicted when it came to Erma. It was always better to simply feel she needed to stay outside a particular zone. One that was far away. But one of the many annoying things about Erma was that she did indeed have useful information sometimes. This was because she inserted herself in everyone's business as much as she possibly could.

Chapter Fifteen

Reluctantly, Myrtle opened the door. Erma delightedly hopped inside, then stopped, glancing fearfully around. "Pasha isn't around, is she?"

Sadly, Pasha wasn't. "No, she's out subduing nature somewhere. Come on in, Erma."

Myrtle was preparing to sit down in her armchair, but Erma looked expectantly toward the kitchen. "Might I have something to nibble on?"

"I suppose so," said Myrtle inhospitably. She was heading toward the kitchen when there was another rap on the front door.

Erma beamed, clasping her hands together. "It's Miles! We can have a sleepover after all!"

"It's the *opposite* of a sleepover," Myrtle grated severely. Did Erma remember nothing? She stomped to the door. At least Miles might be able to help her expeditiously rid herself of her Erma infestation.

But it was Red. He looked tired, but nosy. "Just drove home. Saw your lights on, Mama. And saw you open the door to someone who didn't look like Miles."

He raised his eyebrows as Erma waved excitedly to him from the kitchen. He waved back and murmured to his mother, "Wow, Mama. I'm surprised to see Erma here. Did you get over your phobia?"

"I didn't," snarled Myrtle. She stomped toward the kitchen again and Red followed her, greeting Erma and settling down at the table.

"I shouldn't be hungry," said Red, patting his stomach. "Elaine has been feeding me tons of carbs. Somehow, though, the more carbs I eat, the hungrier I get."

Erma beamed at him. "There's some sort of science to that, I think. Of course, for me, whenever I eat carbs, I get a terrible digestive disturbance. If I eat too much sugar? Or gluten? My guts just . . ."

Myrtle put her hands over her ears. "Enough, Erma! I can't handle medical talk at this time of night."

Erma switched gears quickly. "So, Red, why are you getting home so late? Something to do with the case?"

Red nodded tiredly. "Well, who knows if it's to do with the case, but it was a late call. I might as well tell you because it'll be sure to be all over town tomorrow anyway. Liam Hudson is dead."

Erma tried to keep a handle on her expression, but completely without success. She attempted a look of horror and sadness, but a gleeful grin at knowing something before anyone else did took over. "How awful! And was it murder?"

Red said, "I can't say anything else about it." He paused. "Just wondering what made you decide to come by?"

Erma said, "Well, I couldn't sleep. I'm on this medicine, see."

Myrtle made a strangled sound and Erma gave an apologetic giggle. "Sorry, sorry. I know, no medical stuff. Any-hoo, it keeps me from sleeping. I hate being alone when I can't sleep because it makes me feel like I'm the only person in the world who isn't asleep. So I walked over to see if there were lights on at Myrtle's and there *were*."

She beamed at Myrtle, who gave her a wilted smile in response. "And the thing about Myrtle is that she's so used to insomnia, that she makes it seem fun."

Red said sternly, "It's not fun and it really shouldn't be viewed that way, Erma."

Erma, however, still looked rather wistful, although she nodded.

"It's in fact a dangerous medical condition resulting in car accidents." Red's face was severe.

"I don't own a car," said Myrtle with a shrug.

"Poor decision-making," added Red, ticking off his points on his fingers.

"I'm *always* judicial," said Myrtle.

"And shortened lifespan," finished Red.

Myrtle snorted at this.

Erma nodded eagerly, "You're right. Of course, you're right! That's why it's good this is just a temporary problem for me."

Myrtle said tiredly, "Erma, you did say that you had some sort of information for me." At this point, she didn't even care if Red heard it. She just wanted them both gone from her house as quickly as humanly possible.

Erma looked coy. "Well, I don't know if what I know is very *useful*. Sometimes I just pick things up around town. You know how it is. You get to talking to people and the next thing you know, you find out all sorts of things." She cast a longing look at one of Elaine's leftover biscuits on the counter.

"The information," repeated Myrtle through gritted teeth. She shoved one of the biscuits at Erma.

Erma quickly devoured the biscuit before answering. This was a blessing since Myrtle had no desire to witness Erma trying to speak with a full mouth. Erma brushed the crumbs from her lips and said, "So, Pansy."

Red said, "Pansy Denham."

Erma fluttered her lashes at Red. "Darren's girl, yes. Anyway, I think she's in rather desperate financial straits. And I feel just awful, Myrtle, because we had that big food signup at book club for the next meeting and she probably felt as if she had to sign up for all sorts of things she couldn't even afford! And she's having such a difficult time anyway with her beau being murdered and such."

Red nodded. Myrtle sighed. Red really shouldn't encourage Erma. Any signs of encouragement may make Erma rattle on incoherently for hours.

He said, "And what makes you think she's in such bad trouble financially?"

Erma's eyes grew big. "Oh, it's very easy to see! There's been a real decline in her fortunes, no doubt about it. She used to buy fancy high heels all the time. You'd never see her in the same pair of shoes twice. And at book club, she was wearing a really tired pair of fake leather Mary Janes. Did you notice, Myrtle?"

"No." Myrtle herself wore very sensible orthopedic shoes and rarely noticed or cared about the footwear of others.

"Well, it was quite extraordinary. And it told me a *couple* of things." Here Erma looked expectantly at Myrtle and Red, waiting for them to prod her to disclose her findings.

Myrtle didn't play along.

Red somewhat grudgingly (it was very late, after all) asked, "What did it tell you, Erma?"

"It told me that not only was she in such poor financial health that she was wearing what looked like second-hand shoes, but that she didn't have *all those* shoes she'd purchased in the past. Because why would you wear a pair of shoes like *that* when you could wear one of the dozens of fancy shoes you had in your closet?"

Red was still trying to piece together Erma's thought process with the shoe thing. "So what do you think happened to those shoes? She returned them?"

Myrtle gave Red a pitying look. "Red, you can't return shoes that have been worn. They'd be scuffed."

"No, she'd have had to have *sold* them," said Erma triumphantly, making her hopefully-final point. "And you can do that so many places online. She must have sold all those shoes to try to get money to eat!"

Red patiently asked, "You think she's having trouble paying for food?"

"Of course she is! I've seen her in the Piggly-Wiggly myself and she's simply loaded down with coupons and counting out loose change in the checkout line. No one wants to stand in line behind her because she takes so long to pay."

Red nodded encouragingly again and Myrtle shot him a look, which seemed to puzzle Red. "Okay, Erma. Got it."

"And I promised I'd loan her my library copy of the graphic novel we're reading this month because she didn't want to buy it." Erma grinned with a complete lack of modesty at her altruism.

"Good for you," said Myrtle. "And now, not to be rude, but I'm going to ask both of you to leave. I need to get some sleep."

"Subtle, Mama." Red stood up and said to Erma, "I'll make sure you make it inside all right."

She fluttered her eyelashes at him again and they finally left.

After her nocturnal visits, Myrtle had a hard time falling asleep. She muttered under her breath at Red and Erma as she tossed and turned in her bed, unable to find a comfortable spot. She finally fell into a fitful sleep right around the time the sun was coming up. Thirty minutes later, she woke again and sullenly gave up and got ready for her day.

Her mood had decidedly not improved by the time Miles ended up at her house. He was also in a very chipper mood, which made Myrtle even more surly.

"You must have slept well last night," growled Myrtle.

Miles said, "Like a baby."

Myrtle said, "You know, actually, babies don't sleep very well at all. They wake up every few hours to eat."

"Fortunately, that wasn't the case. I think I've already put on a pound or two from Elaine's baking."

Myrtle nodded. "Elaine's hobbies are always dangerous, usually just for different reasons." She sighed and looked at the clock. "We should go ahead and head out. I think staying busy today is going to be key for me to power through the day and get done with it."

Miles looked a bit trepidatious. Myrtle in a bad mood was something to behold. "Are you sure you just don't want to try to take a nap? We're not on any kind of schedule here, after all."

"There's no point my trying to sleep in the daytime when I couldn't even do it in the middle of the night." Myrtle glared at her living room, illuminated by the light streaming through her sheer curtains. "You know, this place is seriously dusty. Everything needs to be wiped down and the whole house vacuumed so it doesn't light right back on the furniture again. So, instead of simply wasting my bad mood, I'm going to call Puddin and get her to come out here and take care of this."

"Poor Puddin," murmured Miles as Myrtle found her phone and tapped impatiently on the arm of her chair as she waited for the housekeeper to pick up.

"Puddin," she said peremptorily. "I need your help."

"Back is thrown," said Puddin automatically.

"I need you to catch it then, and put yourself together. This house is a disgrace. Miles agrees with me."

Miles raised his eyebrows as he glanced around the living room. Everything was in its place. He shrugged.

Puddin gave a gusty sigh. "Miz Myrtle, today ain't a good day. Seein' my cousin Bitsy and she and I are gonna go to the movies."

"Maybe Bitsy can help you clean my place up. It would go faster that way," said Myrtle. Bitsy may also be somewhat more motivated than Puddin. Puddin's usual routine was to lackadaisically shove the vacuum around before plopping with exhaustion onto Myrtle's sofa to watch morning game shows.

This idea of enlisting Bitsy seemed to appeal to Puddin. "Yeah. Maybe Bitsy could do it." She paused. "You could pay both of us."

"I certainly could *not*. I want my house clean and I was only making suggestions on how that could possibly take place. I'm paying the same amount regardless of who does it."

Puddin grouchily said, "All right. I'll come around later."

"And I might not be here, so do you still have your key?"

There was another pause. "Yeah."

It didn't inspire confidence. "Make sure you have it before you come over." Myrtle hung up and shook her head. "Complete nonsense. All the time."

Just the same, she felt a little more cheerful. Even more so when Miles suggested that they go to the diner for breakfast. "We're always there for lunch," he said. "I think breakfast there is their best meal of the day."

Myrtle thought fondly of the diner's pecan pancakes with whipped cream. It was practically dessert, although she wouldn't classify it that way since it was on the breakfast menu. The thought of a happy sugar high in her future, complete with the sweet coffee the diner served, made her feel practically jaunty. So it was with a bounce in her step that she followed Miles up Pansy's walkway to her front door.

Miles rang the doorbell and no one answered. He paled a bit, hesitated, then cautiously rang the bell again as if the doorbell might shock him somehow.

They waited for a minute. Myrtle grew impatient, the visions of sugary pancakes no longer dancing in her head. She rapped on the front door and listened for sounds of life.

"I can't do it," said Miles, shaking his head. "I'm no first responder, Myrtle. I simply can't happen upon another body first thing in the morning this soon after the last one."

"Nonsense. Pansy should have the good sense not to be dead right now. It's horrid timing. As I mentioned, she's a fairly silly woman, but she does seem to have reasonable common sense when it comes to timing. I bet you anything that she's either in her shower or in her backyard. Let's check out the backyard."

Miles was relieved she'd suggested checking out the backyard and not the shower.

Myrtle gripped her cane and used it to push down into the somewhat cushy grass as she strode around the side of the house. "Pansy!" she barked as she went. "Pansy Denham!"

Pansy, spotted with what looked like potting soil and holding a spade, greeted them at the gate to her backyard. She looked startled. "Yes? Myrtle? Miles? What is it?"

Myrtle quickly transformed, giving Pansy a sweet smile. "Oh, Miles and I were just in the neighborhood, weren't we Miles?"

Miles gave an apologetic grin. "Yes. That's right."

"Miles was driving by your house and we were thinking that we wanted to share some of Elaine's baked goods with you." Myrtle gave Miles a prompting shove with her elbow.

Miles frowned. "Oops. I left the biscuits and pastries in the car." He hurried off to remedy the situation and Myrtle resumed her sunny smile, beaming at Pansy.

"Sorry about that. Miles can be rather vapid until he's had enough coffee. But how are *you*, dear? Everything going all right? Did you enjoy our little book club meeting?"

Pansy, regaining her composure after being summoned so abruptly from her garden, quickly said, "Oh, yes. Yes. What a lovely group of ladies. And it was so exciting to be talking about *books*."

"Yes," said Myrtle, although the word was imbued with doubt. "I'm sure it was. We were all so glad to have you there."

"And I appreciate the baked goods. Were those Elaine's goodies that were at book club?"

Myrtle nodded, smiling. "They sure were. She makes amazing breads and pies and cakes. The only problem is the amazing calories that come along with them. Red and I are trying to share the wealth with others." She heard the car door close and realized Miles was on his way back. Time to ask any sensitive questions—the type that someone like Pansy may not want to answer in front of someone like Miles. "By the way, and I do hope you won't think this too forward of me, Pansy, but I noticed at the funeral how fond Carter Radnor is of you."

Pansy looked a little flustered. "Oh, I don't know."

"It was completely obvious," said Myrtle firmly.

Pansy paused. "The truth is, Myrtle, that I don't really know what to *do* about it. I mean, he's a very kind man. Of course I was a little uncomfortable with his attentions when I was seeing Darren because I didn't want Darren to think there was anything there."

"And there wasn't," said Myrtle, a slight question in her voice.

"Oh no. No. At least, not on my end. I think Carter, when he was widowed you know, I think he just didn't know what to do. His wife had been his whole life and he'd known her since they were in school together. He was used to living with some-one and didn't know how to live on his own."

"Hmm," said Myrtle. She generally disapproved of people who didn't understand how to live on their own, considering how many years she'd managed to successfully do it herself.

Pansy added helpfully, "And it wasn't just the emotional toll of being without a partner in the house. He'd call me up some-times and ask how to do simple cooking or laundry tasks."

Myrtle grunted at this. She spotted Miles heading toward them clutching the food and gave a quick shake of her head. Miles stopped and proceeded to take a good deal of interest in Pansy's birdfeeders.

"So maybe he just sort of latched onto me in a way," Pansy shrugged.

Myrtle didn't think it sounded like a very wonderful arrangement for Pansy to be enlisted as Carter's household helper. But there had seemed to be something else there, too.

"It seemed to me, though, that Carter is genuinely *fond* of you," said Myrtle.

Pansy nodded slowly. "Yes, I think so. I've just tried hard not to think about it."

"It's not returned, then."

"Goodness, no. I just think of Carter as a friend."

Myrtle said, "Sort of a *needy* friend."

"Yes." Pansy considered something for a few moments and then added, "There is something. I hate to say it because Carter has always been so sweet."

Just the sort of information that Myrtle was itching to hear. "Oh?"

"It's just that Carter has been *different* lately. Not really different with me, but different with other people."

Chapter Sixteen

"Different in what way?" Myrtle felt like getting information from Pansy was like pulling teeth.

"Volatile? Is that the right word? Maybe just cranky. Like I said, it was never with me, but with other people. You know . . . I told you at book club that Carter and Darren had argued right before Darren died." Pansy looked down and blinked when she mentioned Darren's death.

Myrtle hurried her on. For one thing, she certainly didn't want Pansy to dissolve into tears. For another, Miles was starting to look restless near the birdfeeders. Plus, there was a chickadee who appeared to be taking offense at the fact Miles was in its flight path. "That's right. You said they were arguing over you?"

Pansy blushed. "I believe it was about me, yes. Carter didn't think Darren was worthy of me. Silly, of course, but that's what he kept telling me. Darren mentioned something about Carter ranting at him to treat me better."

Myrtle frowned. "*Was* Darren unworthy of you? Did he treat you poorly?" When Myrtle thought of Darren, she thought of a crusty old man occupied with chess and reading. Could he have hidden depths?

"No, no. No, he never treated me poorly. But sometimes, he wanted time to himself." Pansy's voice still reflected the hurt she felt from this. "I didn't ever really understand that. I wanted to spend *all* my time with Darren. I wanted to share everything with him—what TV shows I was watching, what my life was like growing up."

Poor Darren. Myrtle tried to summon a sympathetic look, but had the feeling she was utterly failing in the process. No wonder Darren wanted to escape sometimes. Myrtle felt very much the same way now.

"Once or twice I may have called Carter to complain about Darren," said Pansy, looking a bit regretful. "Thinking back, maybe I shouldn't have done that. But he was always so sympathetic and told me I deserved better, and when I called him, I ended up feeling much better about myself."

"And Carter felt upset at Darren," said Myrtle.

Pansy nodded. "I guess so. But that wasn't the reason I told him about Darren. I just wanted to have a sympathetic ear."

Pansy had gobs of girlfriends she could have told her sob story to. Myrtle found it distasteful that she'd chosen to share it with the man who wanted to be involved with her.

Pansy added slowly, "I was wondering, Myrtle, if there was something you'd heard about. When I came outside to go gardening, my neighbor mentioned to me that she heard from a friend that Liam Hudson was dead."

And such was the gossip trajectory of Bradley.

Myrtle said, "I'm afraid so."

Pansy hesitated. "It's sort of odd, but I saw Carter and Liam together in town just recently. At the diner, which is real close to Liam's office, I think."

Myrtle knit her brows. "Was that odd?"

"It was odd just because Carter didn't seem very happy." She quickly added, "But he's an insurance agent and Liam was a lawyer. They probably just had regular business together, don't you think?"

"Maybe so."

Pansy said, "I'd sort of wondered if maybe Liam had something to do with Darren's death." She gave a short laugh. "Not that I had any proof or anything like that. But you said Darren mentioned him right before he died. And then, with those clippings missing?" She shrugged.

Myrtle was less-interested in this since she already knew about Liam's sketchy past. Liam's death had, anyway, certainly made him less of a suspect. She switched gears. Miles, exhausted with the bird-watching in Pansy's yard, gave her a look and she motioned him over. "Pansy, I did have one thing to ask you. I did, as a matter of fact, have a chance to speak with Liam before his untimely demise."

"Oh?"

"I did. And one thing Liam pointed out was that Darren was dismayed at the friends and family who asked him for money after the sale of his painting." Myrtle gave Pansy an innocent look. "I was surprised to hear that. Do you think Liam was telling the truth?"

Pansy flushed. "Darren and I didn't talk a lot about money."

Myrtle said, "You know, Miles can corroborate that until I found money in a pocket, I was very tight on funds until Friday when my check comes in."

Miles nodded.

Myrtle said, "If anyone understands about money being tight, a retired schoolteacher does."

Pansy gave her a considering look. She sighed. "It's been a lot tighter than it used to be. I had some medical issues a couple of years ago and I didn't think they'd have the impact on my finances that they did. But wow . . . they really knocked me low. So I might have asked Darren to float me a loan just to get some of the bills paid." She frowned. "I'd tried everything else first before I asked him. I sold some of my things. I even took on a part-time job."

Myrtle had a vague recollection of Pansy greeting her at the receptionist desk of the local vet when she'd taken Pasha in for shots.

Myrtle said, "But it didn't get you over the hump? You asked Darren for help."

Pansy said, "I did." She made a face and laughed ruefully. "He didn't take it well. I guess he'd had too many people making pitches for money by that point."

Myrtle asked, "So he was . . . what? Defensive? Belligerent?"

"No. No, just sort of sad. Like he thought everyone was just looking at him like a human wallet instead of looking at him like he was Darren. It's funny, but even though he was turning me down, I ended up feeling sorry for *him*." She shook her head. Then she looked longingly at her row of flowers she'd been weeding.

Miles held up the bags. "Should I just put the breads on the patio furniture?"

Pansy gave him a grateful look. "That would be wonderful. Thanks so much. By the way, I really enjoyed the book club meeting. Everyone was so kind. And it's been a reminder of just how much I miss reading. Reading again is like meeting up with an old friend."

This statement made Myrtle slightly more enamored with Pansy. She said expansively, "I have many *wonderful* books at home that you're more than welcome to borrow. Although I *always* come back for my books."

Miles nodded wryly. "I can attest to that. Just return them within a reasonable amount of time or you'll have an agitated Myrtle on your doorstep."

"Thanks for the offer . . . I'd love to have a few good books to read next. And thanks to the two of you for coming by."

A minute later, they were getting back into Miles's car. "Breakfast?" he asked. His stomach growled on cue.

Myrtle nodded. Then she frowned. "Oh, pooh. I don't seem to have my purse."

Miles raised his eyebrows. "That's quite an omission for you. You're sort of like Queen Elizabeth with that thing—it's always dangling from your arm."

Myrtle was aggravated. "Well, I was dangling the grocery bags of bread so I guess I didn't notice it wasn't there."

Miles's stomach prompted him again to head to the diner. "You could just pay me back later."

"No, no. I want to pay upfront. It's never good to take a loan from a friend. You see how it messed Pansy up."

"It wouldn't be a *loan*. You'd pay me back ten minutes after we left the diner." Miles sighed as he saw the stubborn set of Myrtle's chin. "Never mind. We'll swing by your house for a minute. It's practically on the way."

Soon after, he pulled into Myrtle's driveway and she hopped out, striding to her front door. When she opened it, she was greeted by the sight of Puddin sprawled on her sofa, eating chips and watching a very noisy game show.

The housekeeper's eyes grew wide in her pale face and she struggled to sit up.

"Puddin!" bellowed Myrtle. "I asked you to clean up the mess, not exacerbate it! You're making crumbs go everywhere."

Puddin gave her a resentful look. "Just doin' my PT exercises, Miz Myrtle. Told you my back was thrown."

"What kind of second-rate physical therapist assigns exercises like *that*?" Myrtle gestured to the slouching Puddin.

Puddin said with dignity, "I ain't doin' them right now. They go like this." Then she attempted to demonstrate a movement that twisted her back into such a state that it was sure to be thrown if it hadn't been already.

"Stop," said Myrtle fiercely. "I don't have time right now for any of your nonsense and foolishness, Puddin. You'll turn that TV off and clean up your mess and mine. I'm just here to get my purse."

Now Puddin looked wily. "Where you goin'?"

"To eat breakfast with Miles."

Puddin said, "I could use some food right about now."

"Maybe that will motivate you to finish cleaning my house, if you tell yourself you'll have lunch afterward. Besides, it sure looked like you were having a snack to me." Myrtle grabbed her purse and headed for the door.

Puddin said, "Dusty can't pick me up for two hours, so I got time to kill. That's another reason I'm just hangin' out."

Myrtle gritted her teeth. Puddin and Dusty and their sundry unpredictable vehicles were a frequent issue. "You're not suggesting you come to breakfast with Miles and me, are you?"

Puddin said, "I got money. My dad gave me birthday money. I'll pay for a breakfast biscuit for you, even."

Myrtle frowned. Puddin had a living father? She was a woman of very indeterminate age, but she was now having to re-evaluate her estimate downward. She was quite used to Puddin having birthdays, though. Puddin always seemed to have them several times a year and frequently gave them as an excuse not to work or to ask for small bonuses. She'd certainly never offered to buy Myrtle anything on any of the occasions.

"Besides, I got information for you," said Puddin, a crafty look on her face.

"I'll take you up on your offer, Puddin, but only if you understand when you come back, you've really got to clean this place up. It's as bad as it's ever been."

Puddin glanced around the room and gave a shrug as if she'd seen it worse. Then she struggled to her feet. "Let's go."

"And you've got your purse?"

Puddin waved a threadbare Hello Kitty bag at Myrtle and strode jauntily out the door, her thrown back just a memory.

Miles somehow didn't seem at all surprised to have an additional passenger in his car, much less Myrtle's housekeeper. Perhaps, after the terrible shock of discovering Darren, he'd become immune to surprises. He took off for the diner as Puddin regaled them all with various colorful bits of gossip related to their neighbors' yards and the states of their homes as revealed by Puddin, Dusty, and their coterie of yard and housekeeping friends.

They settled into a booth at the diner and Puddin said expansively to Myrtle, "Get whatever you want!" as Myrtle picked up the laminated menu.

"I thought the offer was limited to a breakfast biscuit," said Myrtle.

Puddin made an airy gesture. "Or somethin' similar." Her face darkened. "Maybe don't get no egg Benedict or nothin' like that."

"Thanks for clarifying my choices," said Myrtle dryly.

The waitress came up and Myrtle ordered a stack of three pancakes, which came in well under the breakfast sandwich price. Miles ordered eggs with a waffle. Puddin went all out with the "lumberjack breakfast," a compilation of biscuits, pancakes, eggs, and sausage. Myrtle sincerely hoped Puddin wouldn't choose this occasion to have a coronary event.

After the food came, Myrtle decided to force a change of subject since Puddin was now starting to ramble about Dusty's unforgiveable unhelpfulness in doing his own laundry.

"Puddin," said Myrtle in as commanding a voice as she could muster. "Tell us the information you have."

Puddin, trying to pivot from Dusty's many shortcomings to the new subject, looked blankly at Myrtle.

"You know," said Myrtle impatiently. "You said you had information for me on the case."

Puddin's face was doubtful. "Are you sure I said that, Miz Myrtle?"

Myrtle scowled at her. "You know very well you told me that."

Miles polished off the rest of his eggs and asked, "Did you know Darren at all, Puddin?"

Puddin puffed up proudly at being the source of information. "Sure, I did. Knew all about him, didn't I? He was a good one."

"What made him a good one?" asked Miles.

"He didn't try to do his own housekeepin'. I mean, he kept his house very tidy, but he also used cleaners." Puddin had clear prejudice against men who attempted to clean for themselves. She did exclude Miles from this group, only because he kept an incredibly neat house and because he occasionally invited Puddin over to clean for him.

"How about Liam Hudson? Did you know him?" asked Myrtle.

"That lawyer?" asked Puddin. She made a face. "Bitsy cleaned for him."

Bitsy was Puddin's cousin and the source of much of Puddin's information. She seemed to be a very canny observer and fond of gossip.

"What did Bitsy have to say about him?" asked Myrtle curiously.

Puddin snorted. "You wouldn't think he'd be messy, would you? Always struttin' around in them suits and ties. But he was. His house were always a mess."

Myrtle gave her a severe look. "This is not the kind of information I was looking for."

Puddin put her nose in the air. "If you know about people's houses, you know about people."

"I certainly hope no one would judge me on the state of my house right now. Because its messiness is due to you, not me."

Puddin continued, scrunching up her face in thought. "Let's see. Them others in your case? Like Tripp Whitley."

Miles frowned. "Orabelle and Tripp have someone to clean for them?"

"Them?" Puddin shook her head. "Not much money there. But people talk about Tripp. Say he drinks too much, sees too many women, and plays loud music in the house sometimes."

"Wine, women, and song," murmured Myrtle.

Puddin gave her a suspicious look.

Myrtle said, "Well, we've recently had a bit of insight into Tripp's problems, so none of that is a surprise. What about Carter Radnor?"

Puddin looked delighted. "Him is caught up in this?"

Myrtle gave a shrug. "Who knows? Just wondered what you knew about him."

Puddin leaned in as if the gossip might spread to the four corners of the diner. "I hear he's goin' with that Orabelle."

"Going with?" Myrtle tried the unfamiliar words on her tongue and shook her head. "What on earth do you mean by that?"

Puddin gave her a resentful look. "Like he's steppin' out with her."

"Dating?" asked Miles, helpfully trying to supply the vocabulary that might move the conversation along.

Puddin nodded vigorously. "Just so."

Myrtle said, "Well, that was fast, if that's true. He seemed to be only somewhat interested in Orabelle just the other day. What else do you know about him?"

Puddin scowled. "Cleans his own house."

"Yes, yes. I know that's an unforgiveable sin in your eyes for men to clean their own houses." Myrtle glanced at Miles. "Present company excluded, apparently. Is there *anything* else of any sort of importance that you can think of? Maybe on Liam? I don't know a whole lot about him."

"Didn't pay his bills on time," chirped up Puddin.

"Didn't he? Why on earth not? I'd think an attorney would have plenty of money to pay bills with."

Puddin's eyes blazed. "Wasn't fair! He didn't pay Bitsy on time. And he was behind on his yard guy and everybody else." Puddin made an expansive gesture to indicate that Liam's home help employees were legion.

Miles frowned. "I wonder what he spent his money on."

"Cars," said Puddin instantly. "Him had a bunch of fancy cars."

Myrtle scoffed. "A bad choice, for sure. Why would anyone want or need fancy cars in Bradley?"

Miles said, "I believe it's considered a viable hobby by some."

"Collecting cars?" As someone who didn't even own a single car, Myrtle had a hard time grasping this concept.

"The cars was old, too." Puddin did not look impressed.

"Old or *classic*?" asked Miles.

Puddin squinted her eyes at him. "Huh?"

"Never mind," said Miles. It would take too much effort to try and explain.

"Well, that's all very interesting," said Myrtle.

"Told you I knew stuff," muttered Puddin as she dug in her Hello Kitty purse. A few moments later, there was a pile of quarters and dimes on the table as Puddin carefully counted out the amount needed to cover the bill.

Miles, glancing at the bill and the pile of change, quickly said, "How about if I cover the tip for the three of us?"

Puddin looked as if the word *tip* was quite foreign to her. Miles hastily put a swath of dollar bills on the coins.

Myrtle said, "Thank you, Puddin. That was a very tasty meal."

"And very good information," prompted Puddin.

"Yes. And now you need to go clean my house. I really won't be able to tolerate it if it stays in its current condition." Myrtle stood up and headed out of the diner.

Chapter Seventeen

In the car on the way back to Myrtle's, Puddin said in a wheedling voice, "You know, Miz Myrtle, it's easier for me to clean if you ain't there."

"I'm sure it is easier. You don't have anyone telling you not to watch game shows instead of vacuum."

Puddin persisted stubbornly, "It ain't easy cleanin' up with somebody staring at you."

Myrtle sighed and looked out the passenger window as if trying to find where her patience had gone. Then she leaned forward. "That's Carter Radnor."

Sure enough, Carter was walking down the sidewalk with a small dog of indeterminate heritage.

Miles glanced over, "Looks like he's headed to the park."

Puddin said craftily, "You could meet him in the park an' ask him questions."

"All right. Miles, let's plan on accosting Carter in the park. Puddin, you plan on making my house sparkle."

This agreed upon, Myrtle and Miles headed to the park as soon as Puddin was dropped off at Myrtle's house. The park was right in the center of downtown and a popular place for the town to gather. It was directly across from an excellent ice cream shop, a happy coincidence many people took advantage of. There was a climbing wall for children, paths to walk on, and benches on which to sit. Myrtle and Miles decided to sit.

"You think Carter will come by this way?" asked Miles as they plopped onto a wooden bench with an excellent view of both the paths and downtown Bradley.

"His car is right there." Myrtle gestured to an elderly Cadillac that was parallel parked yards away.

So they sat and waited. Sure enough, twenty minutes later up came Carter with the little dog.

"Well, hi there," said Carter, pausing in front of them. "I didn't see y'all here before."

"Oh, we decided to hang out after having breakfast at the diner," said Myrtle airily.

The little dog, an odd mixture of a bushy chin, droopy ears, and a wiry tail, came up to Myrtle and sniffed curiously. Myrtle reached out and petted it.

Carter beamed at her. "Crystal has really taken to you, Myrtle! She doesn't take to everyone."

She didn't, in fact, seem to have taken to Miles. Miles gave the dog a wary look and Crystal showed a few teeth.

"Yes, well, animals do tend to be drawn to me." She looked up at Carter and said, "My, you're dressed up for walking the dog."

He turned a bit pink, which made Myrtle raise her eyebrows.

"Ah, I thought I might run into Orabelle here," he murmured, taking great interest in a rather sickly-looking gardenia bush.

"Does Orabelle usually hang out in the park?" asked Myrtle. "I thought she'd be delivering mail now."

Carter next gave a soliloquy on Orabelle's daily schedule and routine involving lunch that made it very clear his interest in her couldn't be too recent.

Miles said, "So you're planning on meeting up with her?"

Carter sighed. "That's the ironic thing. She always follows the same routine. But today, when Crystal and I are all dressed up for Orabelle, she's not here."

Myrtle almost gave him a mini-lecture in what irony actually was. But she decided not to when she saw his dejected expression. Instead, she looked closer at the rather-unattractive little dog who was giving her a snarling smile and saw she did indeed have a bow on.

"Forgive me, Carter, but I somehow thought you'd always harbored a bit of affection for Pansy." Myrtle used her best nosy-but-harmless-old-lady voice.

Carter flushed again and looked away. "To be honest, I'm really angry at myself for pursuing Pansy for so long. Even *you* know about it, Myrtle. The whole town must have thought I was making a fool of myself."

Miles cleared his throat. "I don't think anyone knew, Carter. Myrtle just is very perceptive."

Carter sighed. "Nice of you to try to make me feel better, Miles. But I'm well aware of how obvious I was when I was try-

ing to get Pansy's attention. It was almost like a bad habit I'd fall-
en into and it kept me from seeing the big picture."

"And the big picture has Orabelle in it?" asked Myrtle.

Carter shrugged. "To be honest, I'm not sure. But it's an idea
I'd like to pursue and see where it leads me. She's a nice woman
and has always been very thoughtful. She'd chat with me sometimes when she delivered my mail and I was always so caught up
with Pansy that I didn't really appreciate my conversations with
Orabelle. I'm trying to change that now, if it's not too late."

Myrtle said, "I hope it works out. I do like Orabelle." She
paused and then implemented a radical change of subject. "And
I was so sorry to hear about Liam Hudson."

Carter blinked at the rapid shift in topic. "Liam Hudson?"

"You were friends, I believe."

Carter shook his head slowly. "I don't know him. That is, I
know *of* him. But only that he's a local lawyer."

"You didn't have a recent violent argument with him?"
asked Myrtle sweetly.

Carter colored again, but this time with anger. "What?
Who said I did?"

"I don't really remember," prevaricated Myrtle. Old age was
a useful thing when it came to excuses. People seemed to have
such low expectations of one's capabilities.

"I did *not* have a violent argument with Liam Hudson. I
barely even knew who the guy was. I probably wouldn't have
been able to pick him out of a lineup. Why on earth would I
have killed him?"

Myrtle said, "Well then, that's settled. It sounds like you
were doing something else while Liam was killed. Right?"

"I certainly wasn't killing Liam at the time. But there I go again, not knowing when I might need an alibi. I really need to do a better job with that. I was at home with Crystal. Sleeping. And Crystal is quite the bed hog, too." He looked down and Crystal grinned up at Carter with her snaggle-toothed grin. "So that's it. Crystal is my alibi."

Carter looked glumly around him. "Well, I suppose I should be getting along home. Orabelle is definitely not here. Hope the two of you have a good day."

Crystal trotted ahead of Carter to the car and they left.

Myrtle and Miles sat thoughtfully on the bench, watching him drive off.

"I sure hope he doesn't chase Orabelle as much as he did Pansy," said Miles.

"Ditto. Although I don't have much hope considering what we just saw. He was awfully spiffy looking for his walk in the park."

Miles said, "And even dressed Crystal up."

Myrtle made a face. "Hard to make that dog pretty. But she seems sweet. I guess."

"What now?" asked Miles as Myrtle stood up and balanced for a moment on her cane.

"Now? We head back to my house to make sure the Nefarious Puddin didn't just lounge around and eat up my junk food instead of cleaning up the house."

But Puddin had apparently pulled herself together and done some cleaning before Dusty picked her up. The house, although not exactly sparkling, was definitely a lot better than it had been and even had a light, lemony scent to it.

Myrtle beamed at the dustless surfaces. "Excellent!" She did a quick walkabout and saw that, although not perfect, everything seemed a lot better than it was.

"Have you already done the crossword today?" asked Myrtle.

Miles nodded, but pulled a carefully-folded bit of paper out of his pocket. "I thought I might give the Sudoku a go today, though."

Myrtle raised her eyebrows. "That's adventurous of you. I remember the last time you tackled the Sudoku you said it stymied you."

"Yes, but it was a five-star puzzle. As a novice, I should never have attempted that." Miles settled onto the sofa and took a book off Myrtle's coffee table to put under the puzzle. She handed him a pencil.

"What's the level of the puzzle today?"

"Two-stars. I should be able to handle that," said Miles, although his expression was less than confident.

"Just don't tear the puzzle into tiny bits if you get frustrated like last time. I don't want anything messing up my house from its currently pristine state." Myrtle got out the crossword puzzle book from Perkins to pick up where she left off. She frowned at the puzzle.

Miles asked, "How are your puzzles going?"

"These make the ones in the Bradley newspaper look like children's games. These are cryptic, where the clues are deliberately obtuse and just hint at the answers. Each clue is a puzzle, itself. They might be anagrams or homophones or hidden words."

"But you're an expert at doing crosswords. You'll be fine." Miles scowled at the Sudoku, which was already not cooperating.

"I'm solving them, but it's taking me ages for each one. I'm starting to think Perkins's mother must be a genius."

There was a light tap on the door and Myrtle walked to the door. Peering out the window on the side of the door, she spun and said to Miles, "Orabelle!"

Miles put his puzzle down and stood up as Orabelle came in. She greeted Myrtle and gave Miles a wave when she saw him. "Hope it's okay that I'm running by. I just finished up my mail route for the day."

"Come on in," said Myrtle, opening the door wide. Orabelle settled next to Miles on the sofa. "Can I get you something to drink or eat?"

Orabelle waved the suggestion away brusquely. "No, thanks, I packed a lunch and ate on the route today. I just wanted to drop by to thank you both."

"Thank us?"

"Yes. For being kind to Tripp last night. It means a lot to me." Orabelle hesitated, her hands folded tightly together in her lap. "I don't like to talk about things like this, but you deserve an explanation."

Miles shook his head. "No, we don't."

Orabelle said, "All right, maybe you don't, but I'd like to give you one. I can't really make excuses for Tripp anymore. He's a grown man, not a teenager. I just love him dearly and I hate to see him facing such challenges."

Myrtle watched as Orabelle's eyes misted just slightly before she sternly got control of herself again. Orabelle sniffed loudly and then went on, "You see, Tripp has a problem with drugs. He had an issue when he was a young man, but we were able to get him to a good rehab program and he was able to kick it. But the last couple of years have been tough on him. He got divorced and lost his job and the next thing I knew, he was clearly using again." She shook her head.

Myrtle said, "That must have been very hard for you to witness. As a teacher, though, I saw the way drugs could get their hooks into the students. Tripp isn't alone."

Orabelle gave her a grateful look. She relaxed her shoulders into a slightly less-militant posture. "If anything good came out of last night, it was the fact Tripp now says he'll go back to rehab. Maybe it will work again. After all, it took years for him to relapse last time."

Orabelle gave them a hopeful look and Myrtle and Miles nodded.

Orabelle said, "We can hope, anyway. But it meant a lot to me that you two stayed there, talked to Tripp, and then offered him a ride home. I just feel terrible that I wasn't able to help."

"You were out?" asked Myrtle innocently.

Orabelle shook her head. "No. I was actually at home, playing the piano. I was trying to learn a piece I'm playing in next week's church service. I just about have it, except for this one particular part. I keep playing it over and over again, trying to nail the section." She sighed. "When Tripp went out, part of me was relieved. I knew I could practice the song over and over again without Tripp having to roll his eyes and put his earbuds in."

Myrtle said, "Miles and I were happy to give Tripp a lift. You've raised a fine man."

Orabelle narrowed her eyes as if trying to see if Myrtle was being sarcastic.

Myrtle continued, "You really have. Anyone can get addicted to drugs or alcohol. But Tripp is also a pleasant person to be around. You just don't know how many annoying people I deal with on an average day. He seems genuinely nice."

Miles nodded in agreement.

Myrtle added, "And he spoke fondly of you. He mentioned you'd always dreamed of traveling, for one."

Orabelle flushed as if a desire to travel was an embarrassing secret being revealed. She said briskly, "Well, it's one of those things on my bucket list. But not something I *have* to do. I'm perfectly content here in Bradley. And in a lot of ways, I've traveled the world from my armchair by reading books. It's certainly an inexpensive way to travel."

Miles cleared his throat. "Tripp seemed to think maybe you'd have *really* liked to travel. That perhaps you approached Darren about it."

Orabelle's shoulders were stiff again and her hands clenched together in her lap. "Tripp is right. I would still love to see Paris. All the books I've checked out from the library about France seem to just have whetted my appetite. I did go speak with Darren because I thought maybe he and I could go on a trip together. He made so much money from the sale of that painting and he wasn't a young man. I figured maybe he'd be just as interested in seeing the world as I was."

Miles gave her a sad look. "But he wasn't, was he?"

Orabelle shook her head. "No."

Miles said thoughtfully, "Darren always did seem like a homebody to me. He was so happy to stay inside and play chess or read a book."

"He turned me down right away. And I understood . . . in a way. Darren has never really been the big adventurer. I remember being amazed when he ended up in Boston years ago. Of course, he ended up right back here in Bradley. I thought it would be good for him, though, to get out of town and go on a trip—by himself, if that's what he wanted. But he was being fiercely protective of the money he'd made." She shook her head again. "Maybe he hadn't completely wrapped his head around the fact that he *had* money now. He was never one to make rash decisions. I think he wanted time to absorb the knowledge that he was financially secure and decide what to do next."

Orabelle gave a harsh laugh. "And the ironic thing was that he didn't have any time left to reflect. It wasn't fair."

"Did Darren leave you his estate?" asked Myrtle.

Orabelle nodded. "For the most part. And now the fact that I'll be able to travel after all doesn't even make me happy. It sort of leaves me with a bitter taste in my mouth." She paused. "It makes me sad."

"Did Darren also provide for Tripp?" Myrtle asked.

Orabelle said, "No. I guess he wanted me to dole out any money to Tripp. I'm sure he was worried about Tripp's addiction problems and didn't want to do anything to make them worse." She paused. "He did leave some money for Pansy, too."

"Really?" Myrtle and Miles chimed in together.

Orabelle smiled. "Darren always was a bit of a romantic. It's not a huge amount, but it's something. He always had a soft spot for a damsel in distress."

Miles asked, "Is that what Pansy is?"

"I suppose *Pansy* thinks so. And she was able to make Darren think the same thing. Anyway, like I said, it's not much but it should keep the wolf from her door."

Myrtle said slowly, "I did have a question for you, Orabelle. You know how I hear things sometimes."

Orabelle gave her a weary look. "How can you *avoid* hearing things? You're an active older lady in a gossipy small town."

"Yes. Anyway, I did hear that you engaged in some sort of an argument with Liam. I found that a little unusual. Liam was probably the attorney in charge of Darren's estate, wasn't he?"

Orabelle rubbed her eyes. "Oh, this town. You can see why sometimes I feel I want to escape. Apparently, someone has a bone to pick with me." She suddenly stopped looking tired and started looking cross. "You know, people in Bradley drive me crazy sometimes. But this is one rumor I can nip in the bud with your help."

Myrtle and Miles nodded.

Orabelle said, "It's just that I *might*, after many years, be finally embarking on a new relationship. It's really too early to tell."

Myrtle said with a smile, "We happened to run into Carter in the park before we came here. He was looking very dressed up for a walk in the park."

"So was Crystal," offered Miles. "She had a bow on."

Orabelle chuckled, looking pleased. "As if a bow could make that poor little dog look more attractive. She's sweet, though."

"He happened to mention he was hoping to run across you there. Carter seemed to know your routine very well," said Myrtle.

Orabelle nodded. "I deviated from it today, but only because I wanted to speak with you. Yes, he's the relationship I'm hoping might end up developing into something. He'd also like to travel. Maybe it's not too late to do all the things I put on my bucket list. Anyway, about Liam. I did argue with him, but only because I'd heard he might have something to do with Darren's death."

Myrtle narrowed her eyes. "You mean, that he was responsible?"

"Yes. Although I guess it was sort of a leap. Pansy mentioned Darren might have known something untoward about Liam, although she wasn't sure what or how he even knew. It made me wonder if maybe Liam had felt threatened by Darren somehow."

Miles said, "You're not saying that Darren was threatening?"

"I suppose I mean more that Darren found something out about Liam and Liam felt threatened simply because Darren knew about it. Anyway, I've been quite devastated by Darren's death." She paused and took a deep breath. Orabelle's voice shook just the slightest bit as she said, "Darren was the only family I had left, besides Tripp. He and I were very close. His death hit me harder than I could have imagined. So yes, I went over to see Liam and confronted him."

Myrtle said, "Surely, that wasn't a very wise thing to do, if you thought Liam had killed your brother."

"It definitely wasn't prudent. It's not the sort of thing I'd ordinarily have done. I acted completely on impulse."

Miles asked curiously, "How did Liam react?"

Orabelle snorted. "Oh, he was really appalled. He tried to hush me up, first. I thought for a minute he was actually going to put his hand over my mouth so no one could hear me. Then, as he listened to me, he turned white as a sheet. I have no idea what Darren uncovered, but it must have been major."

Myrtle said, "As a matter of fact, I did a little digging and found out a few things." She filled Orabelle in.

Orabelle said, "Well, no wonder he didn't want anyone to know about his past. And Red is *sure* his death wasn't suicide? It sure seems likely to me that Liam just couldn't stand the public humiliation and decided to leap from the window."

Myrtle said, "Red seemed sure. And Tripp did, too, as a matter of fact."

Orabelle nodded. "That's what Tripp told me. It's all very odd. I guess perhaps Liam made someone else angry with him and that person pushed him out the window." She sighed. "I suppose, aside from the fact his past was about to be revealed, he really *wasn't* someone I could picture killing himself. He was far too fond of himself for that." Orabelle stood abruptly and said, "I'm going to let you two finish up your puzzles. Thanks so much again for being there for Tripp last night. I owe you one."

Orabelle quickly walked to the door and out. Myrtle stared after her.

"Curiouser and curiouser," she said.

Chapter Eighteen

Miles shoved his puzzle away as if eager to put it out of his sight. "I think I want to mull this all over. Just to get things set in my head."

Myrtle glanced at the puzzle. "Or you're trying to escape your Sudoku."

"It really is a bad one."

"You said it was two stars," said Myrtle.

Miles sighed. "Apparently, I'm not quite as adept at Sudoku as I am at crosswords."

"Well, perhaps you can apply your talents to the case before you head home. Let's see. Liam was really our best suspect, but I suppose we can count him out unless we're cursed with two killers in this tiny town."

Miles nodded. "Right."

"So let's start with Liam, our most recent murder. Who might have wanted to do away with our local lawyer?" asked Myrtle.

"Tripp was right there," pointed out Miles helpfully.

"Very true. He was there and he was up to no good. But why would he have killed Liam? Unless Liam was trying to blackmail Tripp."

Miles added eagerly, "And Tripp didn't have any money. Not only is he jobless but he has a drug habit."

"I can't say I understand why Tripp would have called the police, though. Wouldn't he have just wanted to slip away into the darkness? The whole thing looked suspicious, after all."

Miles said, "So who else do we have? Carter? He was arguing with Liam."

"Or not, if we're to believe Carter."

"Orabelle? She was arguing with Liam, too," said Miles.

"But she just explained that. And it sounded like a reasonable-enough explanation." Myrtle frowned. "I feel like there's something there that I'm missing, though. I'll have to have a think about it all later."

Miles was still mentally scrolling through the rest of the suspects. "Pansy?"

"I suppose Pansy might have known Darren left her something in his will. And, by all accounts, Pansy has certainly fallen on hard times."

Miles said, "Maybe Pansy killed Darren and Liam knew it and she had to get rid of Liam, too."

"Although it's a bit hard for me to see Pansy stuffing good-sized men out of office windows," said Myrtle.

"Which takes me back to Tripp. Tripp also needed money and was rejected by Darren. Maybe Tripp, high on drugs, took his anger out on his uncle when he wouldn't give him money.

Then Liam knew something, tried to blackmail him, and Tripp pushed him out of the window out of desperation."

Myrtle sighed. "It certainly makes the most sense. Although I rather like Tripp. And here he is on the cusp of changing his life for the better and having a fresh start."

"It's not like you to be sentimental, Myrtle."

"No, it's not. Maybe it's because I taught him long ago and would like to see him finally make something of his life. He had a good deal of promise in school. Even though he didn't choose friends well and wasn't disciplined, he was smart."

Miles said, "What about Orabelle? We just heard her say she'd had dreams of traveling and didn't have the funds to make it happen. Maybe she acted out when Darren denied her money for carrying out her dreams. After all, hitting someone over the head with a flashlight sounds like an impetuous attack and not something anyone planned out. Maybe it was a heat-of-the-moment thing and then Liam found out and she had to do away with him, too."

"Maybe," said Myrtle. "Although how is Liam finding out all this information in our scenarios?"

"He must have come by Darren's house that morning. After all, Darren mentioned clippings to me and they weren't there when we arrived."

"But why did Liam go there? To retrieve the clippings? That means Darren must have called Liam, as well. It sounds like Darren was a very popular person the morning he died. We have Tripp asking him for money. Now we have a supposed visit by Liam. And Darren reached out to you to invite you over. He must have been fairly *reeling* with visitors," said Myrtle.

"He must have been. And we haven't even talked about Carter yet."

Myrtle made a face. "Carter should have realized how wonderful Orabelle was much earlier. He gets points off for chasing Pansy for far too long. But I suppose he's redeeming himself now."

"So Carter could have gotten a call from Pansy," said Miles. "That morning Darren died?"

"Sure. Or, well, that's a lot to attribute to a single morning. Maybe Pansy called Carter, upset, the night before. Then Carter stews about it overnight, and first thing in the morning he can't stand it anymore and goes storming off to confront Darren."

"Right. To confront Darren over the fact that he doesn't deserve Pansy, that he's being mean to her because Darren simply treasures his alone time." Myrtle snorted. "So you're saying Carter got carried away, hit Darren over the head with the flashlight, and left. Liam sees him or knows something and then ends up arguing with Carter later—maybe pressuring Carter for money. Carter pushes Liam out of his office window to solve the problem. I think Carter's office is even in that same building, isn't it?"

"Most of the offices in town are," agreed Miles.

Myrtle sighed. "There's something there. I just can't pinpoint what it is." She glanced at her crosswords. "I think I'm going to let my subconscious work on it while I struggle through a crossword. Want to join me? I'm going to sit in my backyard."

Miles stood up. "No, I think I need to turn my mind *totally* off. I'm going to head home and watch something mindless on TV. Once I can figure out what show actually qualifies as vapid enough. I'm not sure I've watched anything truly mindless be-fore."

"Well, give Puddin a call. She's sure to be able to give you the lowdown in terms of what stupid shows she recommends."

Once Miles left, Myrtle sat outdoors. As she thought through the cryptic clues for the puzzle she was working on, her gaze drifted around her yard and the slope heading down to the lake. Dusty had either pulled out a few gnomes for her backyard enjoyment, or had simply run out of steam and never transport-ed them the rest of the way to the front yard.

She filled in an answer on the crossword and then glanced around the yard again. Wanda was right about those weeds. They were encroaching on her yard from Erma's. And Dusty had obviously completely forgotten her request to spray. There were also dandelions which were about as tough as kudzu to get rid of. Myrtle scowled at the weeds. She thought about spraying them while her mind was on them, but realized the sun was too low in the sky. The last thing she wanted was for Erma's lack-adaisical attitude toward weeds to result in a sprained ankle on Myrtle's part by taking a misstep in the yard. Annoyed, she took a deep breath and turned her attention back to the puzzle.

After a few minutes, Pasha came up to her with a purr. She'd apparently been hanging out in the middle of a row of hostas. The black cat rubbed against Myrtle's leg and then gave Myrtle a fetching look.

"Brilliant Pasha!" crooned Myrtle. "You want a snack, don't you?"

The cat's eyes danced in response.

"Let's go inside and open up some tuna," said Myrtle. On the way in, she brought in the weed sprayer as a reminder to call Dusty the next day.

Pasha ate all the tuna Myrtle put out while Myrtle answered several more clues on the puzzle. Then the cat decided to curl up in Myrtle's lap in the living room. This was an occasional, but always unexpected treat from the feral animal. Myrtle turned on the television and pulled up her recorded shows. There was a British police series that seemed good.

However, the series was *too* good and Myrtle was far too comfortable in the chair with Pasha's furry warmth. The hours passed and Myrtle watched show after show. She was convinced she knew the identity of the show's murder and was determined to watch until they uncovered the truth and her suspicion was finally validated.

So it was quite late and Myrtle was quite startled when there was a knock on the door. Myrtle frowned, pulling her robe closer around her as she headed to the door.

Pasha was even more startled and instantly hopped down, fur puffing out. Her eyes narrowed at the door.

"It's probably Miles," Myrtle said in a comforting voice to the cat. Pasha crept over to stand behind a chair and peered menacingly from the side. It didn't bode well for Miles, if it was indeed Miles at the door.

But it wasn't. It was Pansy.

Myrtle hesitated and then opened the door just a crack. First Erma, now Pansy. Really, it was unforgiveable that people were trying to horn in on her insomnia.

Pansy winced and smiled at her apologetically. "Sorry, Myrtle. I couldn't sleep tonight and decided to go for a walk. I saw all your lights were on and know you frequently stay up late."

Myrtle said with dignity, "I don't stay up late. I have insomnia." Although tonight was definitely a case of staying up late, Pansy didn't need to know that. "And I'm terribly sorry, Pansy, but I was just about to try to turn in." Behind her, Pasha gave a low growl and a shiver went up Myrtle's spine.

Pansy said brightly, "Oh, this will only take a second, I promise. I'd just love to borrow that book you mentioned. You know, now that I'm getting back into reading after all this time."

Myrtle raised her eyebrows. "I'm not sure that I mentioned a *specific* book. Just that I had a lot of good ones. But finding one that will be a good match for you may take time and tomorrow would be better for that." She glanced through the door at the darkness beyond. "You're really very brave to be walking around out there with a murderer on the loose." Although Myrtle nearly substituted *stupid* for *brave*.

Pansy shrugged and said, "I guess, although I feel better holding this flashlight. After Darren died, I went right to the hardware store and purchased one. It hadn't occurred to me that flashlights could be used to protect oneself."

Myrtle shoved at the door to close it. No one knew what the weapon was. But Pansy shoved back, as hard as she could and pushed her way inside.

Pasha gave a low, moaning growl again.

Pansy said cheerfully, "Myrtle, you're acting quite menacing. I have to wonder what's behind that."

"What's behind that is crankiness at not being able to turn in. I'll be back to my lovely, amiable self tomorrow." Myrtle put her hands on her hips.

Pansy said, "It's just that I had a revelation earlier, after we spoke. And, of course, just now, too."

In Pansy's still-cheery voice, Myrtle heard a note of intimidation.

"Did you?" asked Myrtle. She moved toward the front door, but Pansy blocked her way.

"I did. I mentioned something about the clippings and I saw an odd expression cross your face. It took me a while to decipher it."

"Was it boredom?" asked Myrtle sweetly.

"No. It was . . . insight."

Myrtle suddenly realized what had slipped her mind earlier. "Because you mentioned the clippings but I never mentioned clippings to you: just that Darren had told Miles that he knew something about Liam. Only the person who killed Darren would have known that."

Pansy smiled at her. "I don't know why people always underestimate you, Myrtle. You're the smartest person in this little town. That's exactly what I realized you'd gleaned from our conversation, even if you didn't immediately realize it, yourself."

Myrtle glanced across the room at her phone.

Pansy pushed her in front of her toward the phone until Pansy got her hands on it. "You're looking for this, Myrtle? Here, let me take it."

Pansy submerged it into Myrtle's glass of ice tea while Myrtle fumed. Pansy gave her an innocent smile and then tipped her head back in a laugh.

Pasha, either upset by Pansy pushing Myrtle or upset by the shrillness laugh, launched herself, spitting and hissing, claws extended, at Pansy.

Chapter Nineteen

Pansy shrieked and stooped over trying to remove the black cat from her leg.

Myrtle, looking for a weapon of any kind, latched onto the large bottle of weed-killer and swung it at Pansy as hard as she could. Pansy went down with a thud.

The front door swung violently open and Red plowed into the house. "Mama?" he called.

Red stopped short at the scene in front of him: Pasha, fur still puffy and attached to Pansy, Pansy unconscious on the living room floor, and his octogenarian mother hovering threateningly over her unexpected guest's body with a large sprayer of weed killer.

Pansy was checked out by an EMT and then taken away by the state police. Miles, looking rather disheveled but wearing his usual khakis and button-down shirt, arrived after hearing all the commotion on the street and made himself useful by making coffee.

Soon Perkins, Red, Miles, and Myrtle were sitting at the kitchen table with cups of coffee.

"I didn't see any decaf," said Miles apologetically.

"I think we're all up for the day at this point," said Red dryly. "Even if I *wanted* to sleep, I know I wouldn't be able to after hearing whatever frightening tale my mother is about to tell."

Myrtle said, "Now, Red. You're acting as if this is all my fault. Pansy was the instigator. She showed up at my house and forced her way in."

Perkins asked, "Did she even have a premise for her visit or was she immediately threatening?"

"I found her threatening right off the bat. I mean, who insists on coming in when an old lady states she wants nothing more than to go to bed? But yes, she did have a premise of sorts. She said she hadn't been able to sleep, went for a drive, saw my lights on, and remembered I'd mentioned having a wonderful library of books."

Red said, "She said she wanted to borrow a book?"

"Yes. But in reality, she realized she'd slipped up when she and I had been talking earlier. Pansy had mentioned Darren's clippings being missing. But the only way Pansy would have known that is if she'd been there after Darren called Miles."

Perkins nodded. "You made the connection. Then Pansy realized you'd made it and came over to eliminate a loose end."

Myrtle made a face and reluctantly admitted, "I didn't *really* make a connection. That is, I did, but I didn't understand what it meant until I saw Pansy. But it all makes sense. She gave herself away before that, though. I mentioned she was brave for going for a walk in the middle of the night and Pansy said the flashlight gave her confidence because now she realized it could be used for protection."

Miles said slowly, "So Pansy killed Darren . . . because she knew he was leaving her money in his will?"

Myrtle said, "Well, I didn't have much of a chance to speak with Pansy before I knocked her unconscious with the weed-killer bottle. But here's what I think: Pansy needed money. Pansy was used to getting what she wanted. Pansy asked Darren for money and Darren refused. Pansy lost it and hit Darren over the head with the flashlight."

Red glanced over at Perkins and Perkins gave a slight nod. Red said, "As a matter of fact, Mama, you're right. Pansy gave us a nice, tearful confession once she came to. Darren turned Pansy down. What seemed even worse to Pansy was that Darren was committing an unpardonable sin."

"Ignoring her," said Myrtle wryly.

"Exactly," said Red slowly. Perkins looked less surprised than Red did that Myrtle drew this conclusion.

Myrtle said, "Pansy said that was the source of their arguments. She'd go crying to Carter Radnor because Darren had prioritized his reading or alone time over time spent with her."

"Darren headed up to his attic as a way of just walking away from their argument. Pansy followed him, still arguing," said Perkins.

Miles cleared his throat and hesitantly said, "Darren did mention that he was spending a lot of time in his attic. It was becoming a sort of refuge for him, I think."

"That would have been helpful to know earlier," said Myrtle reprovingly.

"I only just remembered it," said Miles with an apologetic shrug. "I was focused on the chess and when Darren talked it distracted me. And Darren was a much better chess player than I was, so I was trying to stay sharp. He seemed to be in a reflective mood and was looking through his old scrapbooks and family photo albums and stuff."

Red nodded. "He probably automatically headed up there as an escape from Pansy, guessing she'd just give up and go home. Instead, she followed him, kept arguing, and then struck him with the flashlight."

Myrtle said, "And she had the presence of mind to wipe the flashlight down. She's not as silly as she likes to make out. Then she had to take care of Liam. I suppose he saw her leave in a hurry before he went in."

Perkins smiled at her. "An excellent deduction, Mrs. Clover. That's exactly how it happened."

Myrtle looked pleased. "Yes. Liam had come by to collect those clippings. Darren clearly phoned him. He must have knocked, not heard an answer, then let himself in. When he saw the attic steps, he must have gone up. Although I'm not sure why he wouldn't have left prints everywhere."

Red said, "He obviously wore gloves or was careful not to touch anything. He didn't have time to wipe everything down before you and Miles came over. Maybe he'd come prepared to take the clippings forcefully if needed."

Miles said, "Maybe he'd intended on killing Darren, himself. He definitely had a reason to."

Myrtle said, "So he went up into the attic, gloves on or being careful not to touch anything, saw Darren's body, grabbed the clippings, and left. But he decided to blackmail Pansy, figuring she must have murdered Darren."

"Which didn't go over very well with Pansy," said Red dryly.

Perkins said, "Pansy stated that she went over to speak with Liam in his office, as planned. She told him the room was stuffy and he opened the window. She managed to push him out of it while he was leaning forward."

"So the only loose end was you, Mama," said Red.

Myrtle nodded. "And thank heaven for Wanda."

Red wearily rubbed his eyes. "Wanda."

"That's right. She told me to mix up a batch of weed-killer."

Perkins and Miles seemed to be hiding a smile as Red said, "Weed-killer."

Myrtle scowled at her son. "Is there an echo in here? Anyway, Wanda clearly wanted me to have weed-killer on hand so I could use the sprayer as a weapon. She didn't *exactly* tell me to mix it up, but she told me my weeds was bad . . . *were* bad. She's a hero again."

Miles said, "Maybe Erma is a hero, too. For having the weeds to begin with."

"There is *nothing* heroic about Erma, Miles."

Red said, "I'm just glad you hit her with the sprayer instead of spraying Pansy with weed killing chemicals. You could have gotten into legal trouble with that."

"As if I'd put dangerous chemicals in my yard! The mixture is just apple cider vinegar, table salt, and dishwashing detergent," said Myrtle with a sniff. "Pansy wouldn't have been hurt at all. But walloping her with the sprayer probably stung."

"They believe she has a concussion," drawled Red.

"Serves her right," said Myrtle.

Perkins politely said, "I'm just glad you're all right, Mrs. Clover. That was fast thinking on your part, psychic or no psychic." He looked at Red. "I think we have everything we need for now, don't we?"

He and Red stood up. Red said, "Mama, Elaine was cooking all day yesterday, so please run by and grab some breakfast this morning. And while you're at it, pick up something for lunch and supper, too. There are way too many carbs in that house right now." He looked ruefully down at his stomach.

Myrtle said, "I'll be sure to run by later after it becomes a more acceptable time of the day. For now, I think I'd like to head over to Miles's house."

"Do we have plans?" Miles looked surprised.

"We should finish our chess game," said Myrtle. "And then we can work on our puzzles. Because the rest of the day I'm going to be busy writing an article for Sloan on how I took down the murderer who's been terrorizing Bradley."

Red looked prayerfully at the ceiling. "I'd likely use another word. I'm not positive Pansy qualifies as a terrorist."

"You didn't see her before I hit her with the sprayer. She was quite malevolent." Myrtle gave a satisfied smile at the thought of Pansy behind bars.

They headed for the door and Red said, "Don't you want to change first, Mama?"

"Why should I? No one cares. Besides, slippers and a robe make a lot more sense at this time of night than the alternative." She gave Miles's more-formal attire a disparaging look. Red shrugged.

Miles and Myrtle followed Red and Perkins out and Myrtle carefully locked the door behind them.

Red said, "I almost feel as if I should make sure you two get there all right."

Myrtle said, "That's silly, since Pansy is out of the picture. But you can do one thing for me. Distract Erma if she pops out of her house. She's been like a Jack-in-the-box lately."

Sure enough, Erma excitedly hurried out of her house once she saw Miles and Myrtle passing, clearly dying to find out what happened. But Red and Perkins dutifully intercepted her and filled her in while Miles and Myrtle scampered over to Miles's house.

They sat in the living room and were quiet for a few moments, each in their own thoughts. Miles finally said, "So Pansy was the culprit all along. I have to say I'm surprised."

Myrtle shrugged. "Pansy's odd manner helped me realize she was the perpetrator. Who asks to borrow books in the middle of the night, regardless whether the book owner is an insomniac or not? But yes. You know how it is. Sometimes when you're not really trying to think about something, it pops in your head." She nodded her head at the chessboard. "Sort of like that game over there."

Miles frowned and walked nearer to study the board. He carefully picked up several pieces in turn and hazarded moves before just as carefully placing each of them back. He said dryly, "It appears no matter what I do, you'll have me in checkmate."

Myrtle nodded. "I think you'd have noticed that earlier if life hadn't been so busy," she said politely. She could afford to be gracious. She'd won the game.

About the Author

Elizabeth writes the Southern Quilting mysteries and Memphis Barbeque mysteries for Penguin Random House and the Myrtle Clover series for Midnight Ink and independently. She blogs at ElizabethSpannCraig.com/blog, named by Writer's Digest as one of the 101 Best Websites for Writers. Elizabeth makes her home in Matthews, North Carolina, with her husband. She's the mother of two.

Sign up for Elizabeth's free newsletter to stay updated on releases:

https://bit.ly/2xZUXqO

This and That

I love hearing from my readers. You can find me on Facebook as Elizabeth Spann Craig Author, on Twitter as elizabethscraig, on my website at elizabethspanncraig.com, and by email at elizabethspanncraig@gmail.com.

Thanks so much for reading my book...I appreciate it. If you enjoyed the story, would you please leave a short review on the site where you purchased it? Just a few words would be great. Not only do I feel encouraged reading them, but they also help other readers discover my books. Thank you!

Did you know my books are available in print and ebook formats? Most of the Myrtle Clover series is available in audio and some of the Southern Quilting mysteries are. Find the audiobooks here: https://elizabethspanncraig.com/audio/

Please follow me on BookBub for my reading recommendations and release notifications.

I'd also like to thank some folks who helped me put this book together. Thanks to my cover designer, Karri Klawiter, for her awesome covers. Thanks to my editor, Judy Beatty for her help. Thanks to beta readers Amanda Arrieta, Rebecca Wahr, Cassie Kelley, and Dan Harris for all of their helpful suggestions and careful reading. Thanks to my ARC readers for helping to spread the word. Thanks, as always, to my family and readers.

Other Works by Elizabeth

Myrtle Clover Series in Order (be sure to look for the Myrtle series in audio, ebook, and print):

Pretty is as Pretty Dies
Progressive Dinner Deadly
A Dyeing Shame
A Body in the Backyard
Death at a Drop-In
A Body at Book Club
Death Pays a Visit
A Body at Bunco
Murder on Opening Night
Cruising for Murder
Cooking is Murder
A Body in the Trunk
Cleaning is Murder
Edit to Death
Hushed Up
A Body in the Attic
Murder on the Ballot
Death of a Suitor

A Dash of Murder
Death at a Diner
A Myrtle Clover Christmas (late 2022)
Southern Quilting Mysteries in Order:
Quilt or Innocence
Knot What it Seams
Quilt Trip
Shear Trouble
Tying the Knot
Patch of Trouble
Fall to Pieces
Rest in Pieces
On Pins and Needles
Fit to be Tied
Embroidering the Truth
Knot a Clue
Quilt-Ridden
Needled to Death
A Notion to Murder
Crosspatch (late 2022)
The Village Library Mysteries in Order (Debuting 2019):
Checked Out
Overdue
Borrowed Time
Hush-Hush
Where There's a Will
Frictional Characters
Spine Tingling

A Novel Idea

Memphis Barbeque Mysteries in Order (Written as Riley Adams):

Delicious and Suspicious

Finger Lickin' Dead

Hickory Smoked Homicide

Rubbed Out

And a standalone "cozy zombie" novel: Race to Refuge, written as Liz Craig